THE HERMIT
AND
THE WILD WOMAN

&

Other Stories

The Hermit
and
The Wild Woman

&

Other Stories

EDITH WHARTON

TARK CLASSIC FICTION
AN IMPRINT OF

ROCKVILLE, MARYLAND
2008

The Hermit and the Wild Woman & Other Stories by **Edith Wharton** in its current format, copyright © Arc Manor 2008. This book, in whole or in part, may not be copied or reproduced in its current format by any means, electronic, mechanical or otherwise without the permission of the publisher.

The original text has been reformatted for clarity and to fit this edition.

Arc Manor, Arc Manor Classic Reprints, Manor Classics, TARK Classic Fiction, and the Arc Manor and TARK Classic Fiction logos are trademarks or registered trademarks of Arc Manor Publishers, Rockville, Maryland. All other trademarks are properties of their respective owners.

This book is presented as is, without any warranties (implied or otherwise) as to the accuracy of the production, text or translation. The publisher does not take responsibility for any typesetting, formatting, translation or other errors which may have occurred during the production of this book.

ISBN: 978-1-60450-187-2

Published by TARK Classic Fiction
An Imprint of Arc Manor
P. O. Box 10339
Rockville, MD 20849-0339
www.ArcManor.com

Printed in the United States of America/United Kingdom

Contents

THE HERMIT AND THE WILD WOMAN	7
THE LAST ASSET	28
IN TRUST	57
THE PRETEXT	74
THE VERDICT	99
THE POT-BOILER	108
THE BEST MAN	133

THE HERMIT AND THE WILD WOMAN

I

THE Hermit lived in a cave in the hollow of a hill. Below him was a glen, with a stream in a coppice of oaks and alders, and on the farther side of the valley, half a day's journey distant, another hill, steep and bristling, which raised aloft a little walled town with Ghibelline swallow-tails notched against the sky.

When the Hermit was a lad, and lived in the town, the crenellations of the walls had been square-topped, and a Guelf lord had flown his standard from the keep. Then one day a steel-coloured line of men-at-arms rode across the valley, wound up the hill and battered in the gates. Stones and Greek fire rained from the ramparts, shields clashed in the streets, blade sprang at blade in passages and stairways, pikes and lances dripped above huddled flesh, and all the still familiar place was a stew of dying bodies. The boy fled from it in horror. He had seen his father go forth and not come back, his mother drop dead from an arquebuse shot as she leaned from the platform of the tower, his little sister fall with a slit throat across the altar steps of the chapel—and he ran, ran for his life, through the slippery streets, over warm twitching bodies, between legs of soldiers carousing, out of the gates, past burning farmsteads, trampled wheat-fields, orchards stripped and broken, till the still woods received him and he fell face down on the unmutilated earth.

He had no wish to go back. His longing was to live hidden from life. Up the hillside he found a hollow in the rock, and built before it a porch of boughs bound together with withies. He fed on nuts and roots, and on trout which he caught with his hands under the stones in the stream. He had always been a quiet boy, liking to sit at his mother's feet and watch the flowers grow on her embroidery frame, while the chaplain read aloud the histories of the Desert Fathers from a great silver-clasped volume. He would rather have been bred a clerk and scholar than a knight's son, and his happiest moments were when he served mass for the chaplain in the early morning, and felt his heart flutter up and up like a lark, up and up till it was lost in infinite space and brightness. Almost as happy were the hours when he sat beside the foreign painter who came over the mountains to paint the chapel, and under whose brush celestial faces grew out of the rough wall as if he had sown some magic seed which flowered while you watched it. With the appearing of every gold-rimmed face the boy felt he had won another friend, a friend who would come and bend above him at night, keeping off the ugly visions which haunted his pillow—visions of the gnawing monsters about the church-porch, evil-faced bats and dragons, giant worms and winged bristling hogs, a devil's flock who crept down from the stone-work at night and hunted the souls of sinful children through the town. With the growth of the picture the bright mailed angels thronged so close about the boy's bed that between their interwoven wings not a snout or a claw could force itself; and he would turn over sighing on his pillow, which felt as soft and warm as if it had been lined with down from those sheltering pinions.

All these thoughts came back to him now in his cave on the cliff-side. The stillness seemed to enclose him with wings, to fold him away from life and evil. He was never restless or discontented. He loved the long silent empty days, each one as like the other as pearls in a well-matched string. Above all he liked to have time to save his soul. He had been greatly troubled about his soul since a band of Flagellants had passed through the town, exhibiting their gaunt scourged bodies and exhorting the people to turn from soft raiment and delicate fare, from marriage and money-getting and dancing and games, and think only how they might escape the devil's talons and the great red blaze of hell. For days that red blaze hung on the edge of the boy's thoughts like the light of a burning city across a plain. There seemed to be so many pitfalls to avoid—so many things were wicked which one might have supposed to be harmless. How could a child of his age tell? He dared not for a moment think of anything else. And the scene of sack and slaughter from which he had fled gave shape and distinctness to that blood-red vision. Hell was like that, only a million million times worse. Now he knew how flesh looked when devils' pincers tore it, how the shrieks of the damned sounded, and how roasting bodies smelled. How could a Christian spare one moment of his days and nights from the long long struggle to keep safe from the wrath to come?

Gradually the horror faded, leaving only a tranquil pleasure in the minute performance of his religious duties. His mind was not naturally given to the contemplation of evil, and in the blessed solitude of his new life his thoughts dwelt more and more on the beauty of holiness. His desire was to be perfectly good, and to live in love and charity with his fellow-men; and how could one do this without fleeing from them?

At first his life was difficult, for in the winter season he was put to great straits to feed himself; and there were nights when the sky was like an iron vault, and a hoarse wind rattled the oakwood in the valley, and a great fear came on him that was worse than any cold. But in time it became known to his townsfolk and to the peasants in the neighbouring valleys that he had withdrawn to the wilderness to lead a godly life; and after that his worst hardships were over, for pious persons brought him gifts of oil and dried fruit, one good woman gave him seeds from her garden, another spun for him a hodden gown, and others would have brought him all manner of food and clothing, had he not refused to accept anything but for his bare needs. The good woman who had given him the seeds showed him also how to build a little garden on the southern ledge of his cliff, and all one summer the Hermit carried up soil from the streamside, and the next he carried up water to keep his garden green. After that the fear of solitude quite passed from him, for he was so busy all day long that at night he had much ado to fight off the demon of sleep, which Saint Arsenius the Abbot has denounced as the chief foe of the solitary. His memory kept good store of prayers and litanies, besides long passages from the Mass and other offices, and he marked the hours of his day by different acts of devotion. On Sundays and feast days, when the wind was set his way, he could hear the church bells from his native town, and these helped him to follow the worship of the faithful, and to bear in mind the seasons of the liturgical year; and what with carrying up water from the river, digging in the garden, gathering fagots for his fire, observing his religious duties, and keeping his thoughts continually upon the salvation of his soul, the Hermit knew not a moment's idleness.

At first, during his night vigils, he had felt a great fear of the stars, which seemed to set a cruel watch upon him, as though they spied out the frailty of his heart and took the measure of his littleness. But one day a wandering clerk, to whom he chanced to give a night's shelter, explained to him that, in the opinion of the most learned doctors of theology, the stars were inhabited by the spirits of the blessed, and this thought brought great consolation to the Hermit. Even on winter nights, when the eagle's wings clanged among the peaks, and he heard the long howl of wolves about the sheep-cotes in the valley, he no longer felt any fear, but thought of those sounds as representing the evil voices of the world, and hugged himself in the solitude of his cave. Sometimes, to keep himself awake, he composed lauds in honour of Christ and the saints, and they seemed to him so pleasant that he feared to forget them, so after much debate with himself he decided to ask a friendly priest from the valley, who sometimes visited him, to write down the lauds; and the priest wrote them down on comely sheepskin, which the Hermit dried and prepared with his own hands. When the Hermit saw them written down they appeared to him so beautiful that he feared to commit the sin of vanity if he looked at them too often, so he hid them between two smooth stones in his cave, and vowed that he would take them out only once in the year, at Easter, when our Lord has risen and it is meet that Christians should rejoice. And this vow he faithfully kept; but, alas, when Easter drew near, he found he was looking forward to the blessed festival less because of our Lord's rising than because he should then be able to read his pleasant lauds written on fair sheepskin; and thereupon he took a vow that he would not look upon the lauds till he lay dying.

So the Hermit, for many years, lived to the glory of God and in great peace of mind.

II

ONE day he resolved to set forth on a visit to the Saint of the Rock, who lived on the other side of the mountains. Travellers had brought the Hermit report of this solitary, how he lived in great holiness and austerity in a desert place among the hills, where snow lay all winter, and in summer the sun beat down cruelly. The Saint, it appeared, had vowed that he would withdraw from the world to a spot where there was neither shade nor water, lest he should be tempted to take his ease and think less continually upon his Maker; but wherever he went he found a spreading tree or a gushing spring, till at last he climbed up to the bare heights where nothing grows, and where the only water comes from the melting of the snow in spring. Here he found a tall rock rising from the ground, and in it he scooped a hollow with his own hands, labouring for five years and wearing his fingers to the bone. Then he seated himself in the hollow, which faced the west, so that in winter he should have small warmth of the sun and in summer be consumed by it; and there he had sat without moving for years beyond number.

The Hermit was greatly drawn by the tale of such austerities, which in his humility he did not dream of emulating, but desired, for his soul's good, to contemplate and praise; so one day he bound sandals to his feet, cut an alder staff from the stream, and set out to visit the Saint of the Rock.

It was the pleasant spring season, when seeds are shooting and the bud is on the tree. The Hermit was troubled at the thought of leaving his plants without water, but he could not travel in winter by reason of the snows, and in summer he feared the garden would suffer even more from his absence. So he set out, praying that rain might fall while he was away, and hoping to return again in five days. The peasants labouring in the fields left their work to ask his blessing; and they would even have followed him in great numbers had he not told them that he was bound on a pilgrimage to the Saint of the Rock, and that it behoved him to go alone, as one solitary seeking another. So they respected his wish, and he went on and entered the forest. In the forest he walked for two days and slept for two nights. He heard the wolves crying, and foxes rustling in the covert, and once, at twilight, a shaggy brown man peered at him through the leaves and galloped away with a soft padding of hoofs; but the Hermit feared neither wild beasts nor evil-doers, nor even the fauns and satyrs who linger in unhallowed forest depths where the Cross has not been raised; for he said: "If I die, I die to the glory of God, and if I live it must be to the same end." Only he felt a secret pang at the thought that he might die without seeing his lauds again. But the third day, without misadventure, he came out on another valley.

Then he began to climb the mountain, first through brown woods of beech and oak, then through pine and broom, and then across red stony ledges where only a pinched growth of lentisk and briar spread in patches over the rock. By this time he thought to have reached his goal, but for two more days he fared on through the same scene, with the sky close over him and the green valleys of earth receding far below. Sometimes for hours he saw only the red glistering slopes tufted with thin bushes, and the hard blue heaven so close that it seemed his hand could touch it; then at a turn of the path the rocks rolled apart, the eye plunged down a long pine-clad defile, and beyond it the forest flowed in mighty undulations to a plain shining with cities and another mountain-range many days' journey away. To some eyes this would have been a terrible spectacle, reminding the wayfarer of his remoteness from his kind, and of the perils which lurk in waste places and the weakness of man against them; but the Hermit was so mated to solitude, and felt such love for all things created, that to him the bare rocks sang of their Maker and the vast distance bore witness to His greatness. So His servant journeyed on unafraid.

But one morning, after a long climb over steep and difficult slopes, the wayfarer halted suddenly at a bend of the way; for beyond the defile at his feet there was no plain shining with cities, but a bare expanse of shaken silver that reached away to the rim of the world; and the Hermit knew it was the sea. Fear seized him then, for it was terrible to see that great plain move like a heaving bosom, and, as he looked on it, the earth seemed also to heave beneath him. But presently he remembered how Christ had walked the waves, and how even Saint Mary of Egypt, who was a great sinner, had crossed the waters of Jordan dry-shod to receive the Sacrament from the Abbot Zosimus; and then the Hermit's heart grew still, and he sang as he went down the mountain: "The sea shall praise Thee, O Lord."

All day he kept seeing it and then losing it; but toward night he came to a cleft of the hills, and lay down in a pine-wood to sleep. He had now been six days gone, and once and again he thought anxiously of his herbs; but he said to himself: "What though my garden perish, if I see a holy man face to face and praise God in his company?" So he was never long cast down.

Before daylight he was afoot under the stars; and leaving the wood where he had slept, began climbing the face of a tall cliff, where he had to clutch the jutting ledges with his hands, and with every step he gained, a rock seemed thrust forth to hurl him back. So, footsore and bleeding, he reached a little stony plain as the sun dropped to the sea; and in the red light he saw a hollow rock, and the Saint sitting in the hollow.

The Hermit fell on his knees, praising God; then he rose and ran across the plain to the rock. As he drew near he saw that the Saint was a very old man, clad in goatskin, with a long white beard. He sat motionless, his hands on his knees, and two red eye-sockets turned to the sunset. Near him was a young boy in skins who brushed the flies from his face; but they always came back, and settled on the rheum which ran from his eyes.

He did not appear to hear or see the approach of the Hermit, but sat quite still till the boy said: "Father, here is a pilgrim."

Then he lifted up his voice and asked angrily who was there and what the stranger sought.

The Hermit answered: "Father, the report of your holy practices came to me a long way off, and being myself a solitary, though not worthy to be named with you for godliness, it seemed fitting that I should cross the mountains to visit you, that we might sit together and speak in praise of solitude."

The Saint replied: "You fool, how can two sit together and praise solitude, since by so doing they put an end to the thing they pretend to honour?"

The Hermit, at that, was sorely abashed, for he had thought his speech out on the way, reciting it many times over; and now it appeared to him vainer than the crackling of thorns under a pot.

Nevertheless he took heart and said: "True, Father; but may not two sinners sit together and praise Christ, who has taught them the blessings of solitude?"

But the other only answered: "If you had really learned the blessings of solitude you would not squander them in idle wandering." And, the Hermit not knowing how to reply, he said again: "If two sinners meet they can best praise Christ by going each his own way in silence."

After that he shut his lips and continued motionless while the boy brushed the flies from his eye-sockets; but the Hermit's heart sank, and for the first time he felt all the weariness of the way he had fared, and the great distance dividing him from home.

He had meant to take counsel with the Saint concerning his lauds, and whether he ought to destroy them; but now he had no heart to say another word, and turning away he began to descend the mountain. Presently he heard steps running behind him, and the boy came up and pressed a honey-comb in his hand.

"You have come a long way and must be hungry," he said; but before the Hermit could thank him he had hastened back to his task. So the Hermit crept down the mountain till he reached the wood where he had slept before; and there he made his bed again, but he had no mind to eat before sleeping, for his heart hungered more than his body; and his salt tears made the honey-comb bitter.

III

ON the fourteenth day he came to the valley below his cliff, and saw the walls of his native town against the sky. He was footsore and heavy of heart, for his long pilgrimage had brought him only weariness and humiliation, and as no drop of rain had fallen he knew that his garden must have perished. So he climbed the cliff heavily and reached his cave at the angelus.

But there a great wonder awaited him. For though the scant earth of the hillside was parched and crumbling, his garden-soil reeked with moisture, and his plants had shot up, fresh and glistening, to a height they had never before attained. More wonderful still, the tendrils of the gourd had been trained about his door, and kneeling down he saw that the earth had been loosened between the rows of sprouting vegetables, and that every leaf sparkled with drops as though the rain had but newly ceased. Then it appeared to the Hermit that he beheld a miracle, but doubting his own deserts he refused to believe himself worthy of such grace, and went within doors to ponder on what had befallen him. And on his bed of rushes he saw a young woman sleeping, clad in an outlandish garment, with strange amulets about her neck.

The sight was very terrifying to the Hermit, for he recalled how often the demon, in tempting the Desert Fathers, had taken the form of a woman for their undoing; but he reflected that, since there was nothing pleasing to him in the sight of this female, who was brown as a nut and lean with wayfaring, he ran no great danger in looking at her. At first he took her for a wandering Egyptian, but as he looked he perceived, among the heathen charms, an Agnus Dei in her bosom; and this so surprised him that he bent over and called on her to wake.

She sprang up with a start, but seeing the Hermit's gown and staff, and his face above her, lay quiet and said to him: "I have watered your garden daily in return for the beans and oil that I took from your store."

"Who are you, and how do you come here?" asked the Hermit.

She said: "I am a wild woman and live in the woods."

And when he pressed her again to tell him why she had sought shelter in his cave, she said that the land to the south, whence she came, was full of armed companies and bands of marauders, and that great license and bloodshed prevailed there; and this the Hermit knew to be true, for he had heard of it on his homeward journey. The Wild Woman went on to tell him that she had been hunted through the woods like an animal by a band of drunken men-at-arms, Lansknechts from the north by their barbarous dress and speech, and at length, starving and spent, had come on his cave and hidden herself from her pursuers. "For," she said, "I fear neither wild beasts nor the woodland people, charcoal burners, Egyptians, wandering minstrels or chapmen; even the highway robbers do not touch me, because I am poor and brown; but these armed men flown with blood and wine are more terrible than wolves and tigers."

And the Hermit's heart melted, for he thought of his little sister lying with her throat slit across the altar steps, and of the scenes of blood and rapine from which he had fled away into the wilderness. So he said to the stranger that it was not meet he should house her in his cave, but that he would send a messenger to the town across the valley, and beg a pious woman there to give her lodging and work in her household. "For," said he, "I perceive by the blessed image about your neck that you are not a heathen wilding, but a child of Christ, though so far astray from Him in the desert."

"Yes," she said, "I am a Christian, and know as many prayers as you; but I will never set foot in city walls again, lest I be caught and put back into the convent."

"What," cried the Hermit with a start, "you are a runagate nun?" And he crossed himself, and again thought of the demon.

She smiled and said: "It is true I was once a cloistered woman, but I will never willingly be one again. Now drive me forth if you like; but I cannot go far, for I have a wounded foot, which I got in climbing the cliff with water for your garden." And she pointed to a deep cut in her foot.

At that, for all his fear, the Hermit was moved to pity, and washed the cut and bound it up; and as he did so he bethought him that perhaps his strange visitor had been sent to him not for his soul's undoing but for her own salvation. And from that hour he earnestly yearned to save her.

But it was not fitting that she should remain in his cave; so, having given her water to drink and a handful of lentils, he raised her up and putting his staff in her hand guided her to a hollow not far off in the face of the cliff. And while he was doing this he heard the sunset bells ring across the valley, and set about reciting the *Angelus Domini nuntiavit Mariae;* and she joined in very piously, with her hands folded, not missing a word.

Nevertheless the thought of her wickedness weighed on him, and the next day when he went to carry her food he asked her to tell him how it came about that she had fallen into such abominable sin. And this is the story she told.

IV

I was born (said she) in the north country, where the winters are long and cold, where snow sometimes falls in the valleys, and the high mountains for months are white with it. My father's castle is in a tall green wood, where the winds always rustle, and a cold river runs down from the ice-gorges. South of us was the wide plain, glowing with heat, but above us were stony passes where the eagle nests and the storms howl; in winter great fires roared in our chimneys, and even in summer there was always a cool air off the gorges. But when I was a child my mother went southward in the great Empress's train and I went with her. We travelled many days, across plains and mountains, and saw Rome, where the Pope lives in a golden palace, and many other cities, till we came to the great Emperor's court. There for two years or more we lived in pomp and merriment, for it was a wonderful court, full of mimes, magicians, philosophers and poets; and the Empress's ladies spent their days in mirth and music, dressed in light silken garments, walking in gardens of roses, and bathing in a great cool marble tank, while the Emperor's eunuchs guarded the approach to the gardens. Oh, those baths in the marble tank, my Father! I used to lie awake through the whole hot southern night, and think of that plunge at sunrise under the last stars. For we were in a burning country, and I pined for the tall green woods and the cold stream of my father's valley; and when I had cooled my limbs in the tank I lay all day in the scant cypress shade and dreamed of my next bath.

My mother pined for the coolness till she died; then the Empress put me in a convent and I was forgotten. The convent was on the side of a bare yellow hill, where bees made a hot buzzing in the thyme. Below was the sea, blazing with a million shafts of light; and overhead a blinding sky, which reflected the sun's glitter like a huge baldric of steel. Now the convent was built on the site of an old pleasure-house which a holy Princess had given to our Order; and a part of the house was left standing with its court and garden. The nuns had built all about the garden; but they left the cypresses in the middle, and the long marble tank where the Princess and her ladies had bathed. The tank, however, as you may conceive, was no longer used as a bath; for the washing of the body is an indulgence forbidden to cloistered virgins; and our Abbess, who was famed for her austerities, boasted that, like holy Sylvia the nun, she never touched water save to bathe her finger-tips before receiving the Sacrament. With such an example before them, the nuns were obliged to conform to the same pious rule, and many, having been bred in the convent from infancy, regarded all ablutions with horror, and felt no temptation to cleanse the filth from their flesh; but I, who had bathed daily, had the freshness of clear water in my veins, and perished slowly for want of it, like your garden herbs in a drought.

My cell did not look on the garden, but on the steep mule-path leading up the cliff, where all day long the sun beat as if with flails of fire, and I saw the sweating peasants toil up and down behind their thirsty asses, and the beggars whining and scraping their sores in the heat. Oh, how I hated to look out through the bars on that burning world! I used to turn away from it, sick with disgust, and lying on my hard bed, stare up by the hour at the ceiling of my cell. But flies crawled in hundreds on the ceiling, and the hot noise they made was worse than the glare. Sometimes, at an hour when I knew myself unobserved, I tore off my stifling gown, and hung it over the grated window, that I might no longer see the shaft of hot sunlight lying across my cell, and the dust dancing in it like fat in the fire. But the darkness choked me, and I struggled for breath as though I lay at the bottom of a pit; so that at last I would spring up, and dragging down the dress, fling myself on my knees before the Cross, and entreat our Lord to give me the gift of holiness, that I might escape the everlasting fires of hell, of which this heat was like an awful foretaste. For if I could not endure the scorching of a summer's day, with what constancy could I meet the thought of the flame that dieth not?

This longing to escape the heat of hell made me apply myself to a devouter way of living, and I reflected that if my bodily distress were somewhat eased I should be able to throw myself with greater zeal into the practice of vigils and austerities. And at length, having set forth to the Abbess that the sultry air of my cell induced in me a grievous heaviness of sleep, I prevailed on her to lodge me in that part of the building which overlooked the garden.

For a few days I was quite happy, for instead of the dusty mountainside, and the sight of the sweating peasants and their asses, I looked out on dark cypresses and rows of budding vegetables. But presently I found I had not bettered myself. For with the approach of midsummer the garden, being all enclosed with buildings, grew as stifling as my cell. All the green things in it withered and dried off, leaving trenches of bare red earth, across which the cypresses cast strips of shade too narrow to cool the aching heads of the nuns who sought shelter there; and I began to think sorrowfully of my former cell, where now and then there came a sea-breeze, hot and languid, yet alive, and where at least I could look out upon the sea. But this was not the worst; for when the dog-days came I found that the sun, at a certain hour, cast on the ceiling of my cell the reflection of the ripples on the garden-tank; and to say how I suffered from this sight is not within the power of speech. It was indeed agony to watch the clear water rippling and washing above my head, yet feel no solace of it on my limbs: as though I had been a senseless brazen image lying at the bottom of a well. But the image, if it felt no refreshment, would have suffered no torture; whereas every inch of my skin throbbed with thirst, and every vein was a mouth of Dives praying for a drop of water. Oh, Father, how shall I tell you the grievous pains that I endured? Sometimes I so feared the sight of the mocking ripples overhead that I hid my eyes from their approach, lying face down on my burning bed till I knew that they were gone; yet on cloudy days, when they did not come, the heat was even worse to bear.

By day I hardly dared trust myself in the garden, for the nuns walked there, and one fiery noon they found me hanging so close above the tank that they snatched me away, crying out that I had tried to destroy myself. The scandal of this reaching the Abbess, she sent for me to know what demon had beset me; and when I wept and said, the longing to bathe my burning body, she broke into great anger and cried out: "Do you not know that this is a sin well-nigh as great as the other, and condemned by all the greatest saints? For a nun may be tempted to take her life through excess of self-scrutiny and despair of her own worthiness; but this desire to indulge the despicable body is one of the lusts of the flesh, to be classed with concupiscence and adultery." And she ordered me to sleep every night for a month in my heavy gown, with a veil upon my face.

Now, Father, I believe it was this penance that drove me to sin. For we were in the dog-days, and it was more than flesh could bear. And on the third night, after the portress had passed, and the lights were out, I rose and flung off my veil and gown, and knelt in my window fainting. There was no moon, but the sky was full of stars. At first the garden was all blackness; but as I looked I saw a faint twinkle between the cypress-trunks, and I knew it was the starlight on the tank. The water! The water! It was there close to me—only a few bolts and bars were between us.

The portress was a heavy sleeper, and I knew where her keys hung, on a nail just within the door of her cell. I stole thither, unlatched the door, seized the keys and crept barefoot down the corridor. The bolts of the cloister-door were stiff and heavy, and I dragged at them till the veins in my wrists were bursting. Then I turned the key and it cried out in the ward. I stood still, my whole body beating with fear lest the hinges too should have a voice—but no one stirred, and I pushed open the door and slipped out. The garden was as airless as a pit, but at least I could stretch my arms in it; and, oh, my Father, the sweetness of the stars! The stones in the path cut my feet as I ran, but I thought of the joy of bathing them in the tank, and that made the wounds sweet to me.... My Father, I have heard of the temptations which in times past assailed the holy Solitaries of the desert, flattering the reluctant flesh beyond resistance; but none, I think, could have surpassed in ecstasy that first touch of the water on my limbs. To prolong the joy I let myself slip in slowly, resting my hands on the edge of the tank, and smiling to see my body, as I lowered it, break up the shining black surface and shatter the starbeams into splinters. And the water, my Father, seemed to crave me as I craved it. Its ripples rose about me, first in furtive touches, then in a long embrace that clung and drew me down; till at length they lay like kisses on my lips. It was no frank comrade like the mountain pools of my childhood, but a secret playmate compassionating my pains and soothing them with noiseless hands. From the first I thought of it as an accomplice—its whisper seemed to promise me secrecy if I would promise it love. And I went back and back to it, my Father; all day I lived in the thought of it; each night I stole to it with fresh thirst. . . .

But at length the old portress died, and a young lay-sister took her place. She was a light sleeper, and keen-eared; and I knew the danger of venturing to her cell. I knew the danger, but when darkness came I felt the water drawing me. The first night I fought on my bed and held out; but the second I crept to her door. She made no motion when I entered, but rose up secretly and stole after me; and the second night she warned the Abbess, and the two came on me as I stood by the tank.

I was punished with terrible penances: fasting, scourging, imprisonment, and the privation of drinking water; for the Abbess stood amazed at the obduracy of my sin, and was resolved to make me an example to my fellows. For a month I endured the pains of hell; then one night the Saracen pirates fell on our convent. On a sudden the darkness was full of flames and blood; but while the other nuns ran hither and thither, clinging to the Abbess's feet or shrieking on the steps of the altar, I slipped through an unwatched postern and made my way to the hills. The next day the Emperor's soldiery descended on the carousing heathen, slew them and burned their vessels on the beach; the Abbess and nuns were rescued, the convent walls rebuilt, and peace restored to the holy precincts. All this I heard from a shepherdess of the hills, who found me in my hiding, and brought me honeycomb and water. In her simplicity she offered to lead me home to the convent; but while she slept I laid off my wimple and scapular, and stealing her cloak fled away lest she should betray me. And since then I have wandered alone over the face of the world, living in woods and desert places, often hungry, often cold and sometimes fearful; yet resigned to any hardship, and with a front for any peril, if only I may sleep under the free heaven and wash the dust from my body in cool water.

V

THE Hermit, as may be supposed, was much perturbed by this story, and dismayed that such sinfulness should cross his path. His first motion was to drive the woman forth, for he knew the heinousness of the craving for water, and how Saint Jerome, Saint Augustine and other holy doctors have taught that they who would purify the soul must not be distraught by the vain cares of bodily cleanliness; yet, remembering the lust that drew him to his lauds, he dared not judge his sister's fault too harshly.

Moreover he was moved by the Wild Woman's story of the hardships she had suffered, and the godless company she had been driven to keep—Egyptians, jugglers, outlaws and even sorcerers, who are masters of the pagan lore of the East, and still practice their dark rites among the simple folk of the hills. Yet she would not have him think wholly ill of this vagrant people, from whom she had often received food and comfort; and her worst danger, as he learned with shame, had come from the *girovaghi* or wandering monks, who are the scourge and dishonour of Christendom; carrying their ribald idleness from one monastery to another, and leaving on their way a trail of thieving, revelry and worse. Once or twice the Wild Woman had nearly fallen into their hands; but had been saved by her own quick wit and skill in woodcraft. Once, so she assured the Hermit, she had found refuge with a faun and his female, who fed and sheltered her in their cave, where she slept on a bed of leaves with their shaggy nurslings; and in this cave she had seen a stock or idol of wood, extremely seamed and ancient, before which the wood-creatures, when they thought she slept, laid garlands and the wild bees' honey-comb.

She told him also of a hill-village of weavers, where she lived many weeks, and learned to ply their trade in return for her lodging; and where wayfaring men in the guise of cobblers, charcoal-burners or goatherds came and taught strange doctrines at midnight in the poor hovels. What they taught she could not clearly tell, save that they believed each soul could commune directly with its Maker, without need of priest or intercessor; also she had heard from some of their disciples that there are two Gods, one of good and one of evil, and that the God of evil has his throne in the Pope's palace in Rome. But in spite of these dark teachings they were a mild and merciful folk, full of loving-kindness toward poor persons and wayfarers; so that her heart grieved for them when one day a Dominican monk appeared in the village with a company of soldiers, and some of the weavers were seized and dragged to prison, while others, with their wives and babes, fled to the winter woods. She fled with them, fearing to be charged with their heresy, and for months they lay hid in desert places, the older and weaker, who fell sick from want and exposure, being devoutly ministered to by their brethren, and dying in the sure faith of heaven.

All this she related modestly and simply, not as one who joys in a godless life, but as having been drawn into it through misadventure; and she told the Hermit that when she heard the sound of church bells she never failed to say an Ave or a Pater; and that often, as she lay in the midnight darkness of the forest, she had hushed her fears by reciting the versicles from the Evening Hour:

Keep us, O Lord, as the apple of the eye,
Protect us under the shadow of Thy wings.

The wound in her foot healed slowly; and the Hermit, while it was mending, repaired daily to her cave, reasoning with her in love and charity, and exhorting her to return to the cloister. But this she persistently refused to do; and fearing lest she attempt to fly before her foot was healed, and so expose herself to hunger and ill-usage, he promised not to betray her presence, or to take any measures toward restoring her to her Order.

He began indeed to doubt whether she had any calling to the life enclosed; yet her gentleness and innocency of mind made him feel that she might be won back to holy living, if only her freedom were assured. So after many inward struggles (since his promise forbade his taking counsel with any concerning her) he resolved to let her remain in the cave till some light should come to him. And one day, visiting her about the hour of Nones (for it became his pious habit to say the evening office with her), he found her engaged with a little goatherd, who in a sudden seizure had fallen from a rock above her cave, and lay senseless and full of blood at her feet. And the Hermit saw with wonder how skilfully she bound up his cuts and restored his senses, giving him to drink of a liquor she had distilled from the wild simples of the mountain; whereat the boy opened his eyes and praised God, as one restored by heaven. Now it was known that this lad was subject to possessions, and had more than once dropped lifeless while he heeded his flock; and the Hermit, knowing that only great saints or unclean necromancers can loosen devils, feared that the Wild Woman had exorcised the spirits by means of unholy spells. But she told him that the goatherd's sickness was caused only by the heat of the sun, and that, such seizures being common in the hot countries whence she came, she had learned from a wise woman how to stay them by a decoction of the *carduus benedictus*, made in the third night of the waxing moon, but without the aid of magic.

"But," she continued, "you need not fear my bringing scandal on your holy retreat, for by the arts of the same wise woman my own wound is well-nigh healed, and tonight at sunset I set forth on my travels."

The Hermit's heart grew heavy as she spoke, and it seemed to him that her own look was sorrowful. And suddenly his perplexities were lifted from him, and he saw what was God's purpose with the Wild Woman.

"Why," said he, "do you fly from this place, where you are safe from molestation, and can look to the saving of your soul? Is it that your feet weary for the road, and your spirits are heavy for lack of worldly discourse?"

She replied that she had no wish to travel, and felt no repugnance to solitude. "But," said she, "I must go forth to beg my bread, since in this wilderness there is none but yourself to feed me; and moreover, when it is known that I have healed the goatherd, curious folk and scandalmongers may seek me out, and, learning whence I come, drag me back to the cloister."

Then the Hermit answered her and said: "In the early days, when the faith of Christ was first preached, there were holy women who fled to the desert and lived there in solitude, to the glory of God and the edification of their sex. If you are minded to embrace so austere a life, contenting you with such sustenance as the wilderness yields, and wearing out your days in prayer and vigil, it may be that you shall make amends for the great sin you have committed, and live and die in the peace of the Lord Jesus."

He spoke thus, knowing that if she left him and returned to her roaming, hunger and fear might drive her to fresh sin; whereas in a life of penance and reclusion her eyes might be opened to her iniquity, and her soul snatched back from ruin.

He saw that his words moved her, and she seemed about to consent, and embrace a life of holiness; but suddenly she fell silent, and looked down on the valley at their feet.

"A stream flows in the glen below us," she said. "Do you forbid me to bathe in it in the heat of summer?"

"It is not I that forbid you, my daughter, but the laws of God," said the Hermit; "yet see how miraculously heaven protects you—for in the hot season, when your lust is upon you, our stream runs dry, and temptation will be removed from you. Moreover on these heights there is no excess of heat to madden the body, but always, before dawn and at the angelus, a cool breeze which refreshes it like water."

And after thinking long on this, and again receiving his promise not to betray her, the Wild Woman agreed to embrace a life of reclusion; and the Hermit fell on his knees, worshipping God and rejoicing to think that, if he saved his sister from sin, his own term of probation would be shortened.

VI

THEREAFTER for two years the Hermit and the Wild Woman lived side by side, meeting together to pray on the great feast-days of the year, but on all other days dwelling apart, engaged in pious practices.

At first the Hermit, knowing the weakness of woman, and her little aptitude for the life apart, had feared that he might be disturbed by the nearness of his penitent; but she faithfully held to his commands, abstaining from all sight of him save on the Days of Obligation; and when they met, so modest and devout was her demeanour that she raised his soul to fresh fervency. And gradually it grew sweet to him to think that, near by though unseen, was one who performed the same tasks at the same hours; so that, whether he tended his garden, or recited his chaplet, or rose under the stars to repeat the midnight office, he had a companion in all his labours and devotions.

Meanwhile the report had spread abroad that a holy woman who cast out devils had made her dwelling in the Hermit's cliff; and many sick persons from the valley sought her out, and went away restored by her. These poor pilgrims brought her oil and flour, and with her own hands she made a garden like the Hermit's, and planted it with corn and lentils; but she would never take a trout from the brook, or receive the gift of a snared wild-fowl, for she said that in her vagrant life the wild creatures of the wood had befriended her, and as she had slept in peace among them, so now she would never suffer them to be molested.

In the third year came a plague, and death walked the cities, and many poor peasants fled to the hills to escape it. These the Hermit and his penitent faithfully tended, and so skilful were the Wild Woman's ministrations that the report of them reached the town across the valley, and a deputation of burgesses came with rich offerings, and besought her to descend and comfort their sick. The Hermit, seeing her depart on so dangerous a mission, would have accompanied her, but she bade him remain and tend those who fled to the hills; and for many days his heart was consumed in prayer for her, and he feared lest every fugitive should bring him word of her death.

But at length she returned, wearied-out but whole, and covered with the blessings of the townsfolk; and thereafter her name for holiness spread as wide as the Hermit's.

Seeing how constant she remained in her chosen life, and what advance she had made in the way of perfection, the Hermit now felt that it behoved him to exhort her again to return to the convent; and more than once he resolved to speak with her, but his heart hung back. At length he bethought him that by failing in this duty he imperilled his own soul, and thereupon, on the next feast-day, when they met, he reminded her that in spite of her good works she still lived in sin and excommunicate, and that, now she had once more tasted the sweets of godliness, it was her duty to confess her fault and give herself up to her superiors.

She heard him meekly, but when he had spoken she was silent and her tears ran over; and looking at her he wept also, and said no more. And they prayed together, and returned each to his cave.

It was not till late winter that the plague abated; and the spring and early summer following were heavy with rains and great heat. When the Hermit visited his penitent at the feast of Pentecost, she appeared to him so weak and wasted that, when they had recited the *Veni, sancte spiritus,* and the proper psalms, he taxed her with too great rigour of penitential practices; but she replied that her weakness was not due to an excess of discipline, but that she had brought back from her labours among the sick a heaviness of body which the intemperance of the season no doubt increased. The evil rains continued, falling chiefly at night, while by day the land reeked with heat and vapours; so that lassitude fell on the Hermit also, and he could hardly drag himself down to the spring whence he drew his drinking-water. Thus he fell into the habit of going down to the glen before cockcrow, after he had recited Matins; for at that hour the rain commonly ceased, and a faint air was stirring. Now because of the wet season the stream had not gone dry, and instead of replenishing his flagon slowly at the trickling spring, the Hermit went down to the waterside to fill it; and once, as he descended the steep slope of the glen, he heard the covert rustle, and saw the leaves stir as though something moved behind them. As he looked silence fell, and the leaves grew still; but his heart was shaken, for it seemed to him that what he had seen in the dusk had a human semblance, such as the wood-people wear. And he was loth to think that such unhallowed beings haunted the glen.

A few days passed, and again, descending to the stream, he saw a figure flit by him through the covert; and this time a deeper fear entered into him; but he put away the thought, and prayed fervently for all souls in temptation. And when he spoke with the Wild Woman again, on the feast of the Seven Maccabees, which falls on the first day of August, he was smitten with fear to see her wasted looks, and besought her to cease from labouring and let him minister to her in her weakness. But she denied him gently, and replied that all she asked of him was to keep her steadfastly in his prayers.

Before the feast of the Assumption the rains ceased, and the plague, which had begun to show itself, was stayed; but the ardency of the sun grew greater, and the Hermit's cliff was a fiery furnace. Never had such heat been known in those regions; but the people did not murmur, for with the cessation of the rain their crops were saved and the pestilence banished; and these mercies they ascribed in great part to the prayers and macerations of the two holy anchorets. Therefore on the eve of the Assumption they sent a messenger to the Hermit, saying that at daylight on the morrow the townspeople and all the dwellers in the valley would come forth, led by their Bishop, who bore the Pope's blessing to the two solitaries, and who was mindful to celebrate the Mass of the Assumption in the Hermit's cave in the cliffside. At the blessed word the Hermit was well-nigh distraught with joy, for he felt this to be a sign from heaven that his prayers were heard, and that he had won the Wild Woman's grace as well as his own. And all night he prayed that on the morrow she might confess her fault and receive the Sacrament with him.

Before dawn he recited the psalms of the proper nocturn; then he girded on his gown and sandals, and went forth to meet the Bishop in the valley.

As he went downward daylight stood on the mountains, and he thought he had never seen so fair a dawn. It filled the farthest heaven with brightness, and penetrated even to the woody crevices of the glen, as the grace of God had entered into the obscurest folds of his heart. The morning airs were hushed, and he heard only the sound of his own footfall, and the murmur of the stream which, though diminished, still poured a swift current between the rocks; but as he reached the bottom of the glen a sound of chanting came to him, and he knew that the pilgrims were at hand. His heart leapt up and his feet hastened forward; but at the streamside they were suddenly stayed, for in a pool where the water was still deep he saw the shining of a woman's body—and on a stone hard by lay the Wild Woman's gown and sandals.

Fear and rage possessed the Hermit's heart, and he stood as one smitten speechless, covering his eyes from the shame. But the song of the approaching pilgrims swelled ever louder and nearer, and finding voice he cried to the Wild Woman to come forth and hide herself from the people.

She made no answer, but in the dusk he saw her limbs sway with the swaying of the water, and her eyes were turned to him as if in mockery. At the sight blind fury filled him, and clambering over the rocks to the pool's edge he bent down and caught her by the shoulder. At that moment he could have strangled her with his hands, so abhorrent to him was the touch of her flesh; but as he cried out on her, heaping her with cruel names, he saw that her eyes returned his look without wavering; and suddenly it came to him that she was dead. Then through all his anger and fear a great pang smote him; for here was his work undone, and one he had loved in Christ laid low in her sin, in spite of all his labours.

One moment pity possessed him; the next he bethought him how the people would find him bending above the body of a naked woman, whom he had held up to them as holy, but whom they might now well take for the secret instrument of his undoing; and beholding how at her touch all the slow edifice of his holiness was demolished, and his soul in mortal jeopardy, he felt the earth reel round him and his sight grew red.

Already the head of the procession had entered the glen, and the stillness shook with the great sound of the *Salve Regina*. When the Hermit opened his eyes once more the air was quivering with thronged candle-flames, which glittered on the gold thread of priestly vestments, and on the blazing monstrance beneath its canopy; and close above him was bent the Bishop's face.

The Hermit struggled to his knees.

"My Father in God," he cried, "behold, for my sins I have been visited by a demon—" But as he spoke he perceived that those about him no longer heeded him, and that the Bishop and all his clergy had fallen on their knees about the pool. Then the Hermit, following their gaze, saw that the brown waters of the pool covered the Wild Woman's limbs as with a garment, and that about her floating head a great light floated; and to the utmost edges of the throng a cry of praise went up, for many were there whom the Wild Woman had healed and comforted, and who read God's mercy in this wonder. But fresh fear fell on the Hermit, for he had cursed a dying saint, and denounced her aloud to all the people; and this new anguish, coming so close upon the other, smote down his weakened frame, so that his limbs failed him and he sank once more to the ground.

Again the earth reeled about him, and the bending faces grew remote; but as he forced his weak voice once more to proclaim his sins he felt the blessed touch of absolution, and the holy oils of the last voyage laid on his lips and eyes. Peace returned to him then, and with it a great longing to look once more upon his lauds, as he had dreamed of doing at his last hour; but he was too far gone to make this longing known, and so tried to banish it from his mind. Yet in his weakness the wish held him, and the tears ran down his face.

Then, as he lay there, feeling the earth slip from under him, and the Everlasting Arms replace it, he heard a great peal of voices that seemed to come down from the sky and mingle with the singing of the throng; and the words of the chant were the words of his own lauds, so long hidden in the secret of his breast, and now rejoicing above him through the spheres. And his soul rose on the chant, and soared with it to the seat of mercy.

THE LAST ASSET

I

"THE devil!" Paul Garnett exclaimed as he re-read his note; and the dry old gentleman who was at the moment his only neighbour in the quiet restaurant they both frequented, remarked with a smile: "You don't seem particularly annoyed at meeting him."

Garnett returned the smile. "I don't know why I apostrophized him, for he's not in the least present—except inasmuch as he may prove to be at the bottom of anything unexpected."

The old gentleman who, like Garnett, was an American, and spoke in the thin rarefied voice which seems best fitted to emit sententious truths, twisted his lean neck toward the younger man and cackled out shrewdly: "Ah, it's generally a woman who is at the bottom of the unexpected. Not," he added, leaning forward with deliberation to select a tooth-pick, "that that precludes the devil's being there too."

Garnett uttered the requisite laugh, and his neighbour, pushing back his plate, called out with a perfectly unbending American intonation: "Gassong! L'addition, silver play."

His repast, as usual, had been a simple one, and he left only thirty centimes in the plate on which his account was presented; but the waiter, to whom he was evidently a familiar presence, received the tribute with Latin affability, and hovered helpfully about the table while the old gentleman cut and lighted his cigar.

"Yes," the latter proceeded, revolving the cigar meditatively between his thin lips, "they're generally both in the same hole, like the owl and the prairie-dog in the natural history books of my youth. I believe it was all a mistake about the owl and the prairie-dog, but it isn't about the unexpected. The fact is, the unexpected *is* the devil—the sooner you find that out, the happier you'll be." He leaned back, tilting his smooth bald head against the blotched mirror behind him, and rambling on with gentle garrulity while Garnett attacked his omelet.

"Get your life down to routine—eliminate surprises. Arrange things so that, when you get up in the morning, you'll know exactly what is going to happen to you during the day—and the next day and the next. I don't say it's funny—it ain't. But it's better than being hit on the head by a brick-bat. That's why I always take my meals at this restaurant. I know just how much onion they put in things—if I went to the next place I shouldn't. And I always take the same streets to come here—I've been doing it for ten years now. I know at which crossings to look out—I know what I'm going to see in the shop-windows. It saves a lot of wear and tear to know what's coming. For a good many years I never did know, from one minute to another, and now I like to think that everything's cut-and-dried, and nothing unexpected can jump out at me like a tramp from a ditch."

He paused calmly to knock the ashes from his cigar, and Garnett said with a smile: "Doesn't such a plan of life cut off nearly all the possibilities?"

The old gentleman made a contemptuous motion. "Possibilities of what? Of being multifariously miserable? There are lots of ways of being miserable, but there's only one way of being comfortable, and that is to stop running round after happiness. If you make up your mind not to be happy there's no reason why you shouldn't have a fairly good time."

"That was Schopenhauer's idea, I believe," the young man said, pouring his wine with the smile of youthful incredulity.

"I guess he hadn't the monopoly," responded his friend. "Lots of people have found out the secret—the trouble is that so few live up to it."

He rose from his seat, pushing the table forward, and standing passive while the waiter advanced with his shabby overcoat and umbrella. Then he nodded to Garnett, lifted his hat politely to the broad-bosomed lady behind the desk, and passed out into the street.

Garnett looked after him with a musing smile. The two had exchanged views on life for two years without so much as knowing each other's names. Garnett was a newspaper correspondent whose work kept him mainly in London, but on his periodic visits to Paris he lodged in a dingy hotel of the Latin Quarter, the chief merit of which was its nearness to the cheap and excellent restaurant where the two Americans had made acquaintance. But Garnett's assiduity in frequenting the place arose, in the end, less from the excellence of the food than from the enjoyment of his old friend's conversation. Amid the flashy sophistications of the Parisian life to which Garnett's trade introduced him, the American sage's conversation had the crisp and homely flavor of a native dish—one of the domestic compounds for which the exiled palate is supposed to yearn. It was a mark of the old man's impersonality that, in spite of the interest he inspired, Garnett had never got beyond idly wondering who he might be, where he lived, and what his occupations were. He was presumably a bachelor—a man of family ties, however relaxed, though he might have been as often absent from home would not have been as regularly present in the same place—and there was about him a boundless desultoriness which renewed Garnett's conviction that there is no one on earth as idle as an American who is not busy. From certain allusions it was plain that he had lived many years in Paris, yet he had not taken the trouble to adapt his tongue to the local inflections, but spoke French with the accent of one who has formed his conception of the language from a phrase-book.

The city itself seemed to have made as little impression on him as its speech. He appeared to have no artistic or intellectual curiosities, to remain untouched by the complex appeal of Paris, while preserving, perhaps the more strikingly from his very detachment, that odd American astuteness which seems the fruit of innocence rather than of experience. His nationality revealed itself again in a mild interest in the political problems of his adopted country, though they appeared to preoccupy him only as illustrating the boundless perversity of mankind. The exhibition of human folly never ceased to divert him, and though his examples of it seemed mainly drawn from the columns of one exiguous daily paper, he found there matter for endless variations on his favorite theme. If this monotony of topic did not weary the younger man, it was because he fancied he could detect under it the tragic implication of the fixed idea—of some great moral upheaval which had flung his friend stripped and starving on the desert island of the little cafe where they met. He hardly knew wherein he read this revelation—whether in the resigned shabbiness of the sage's dress, the impartial courtesy of his manner, or the shade of apprehension which lurked, indescribably, in his guileless yet suspicious eye. There were moments when Garnett could only define him by saying that he looked like a man who had seen a ghost.

II

AN apparition almost as startling had come to Garnett himself in the shape of the mauve note received from his *concierge* as he was leaving the hotel for luncheon.

Not that, on the face of it, a missive announcing Mrs. Sam Newell's arrival at Ritz's, and her need of his presence there that afternoon at five, carried any special mark of the portentous. It was not her being at Ritz's that surprised him. The fact that she was chronically hard up, and had once or twice lately been so brutally confronted with the consequences as to accept—indeed solicit—a loan of five pounds from him: this circumstance, as Garnett knew, would never be allowed to affect the general tenor of her existence. If one came to Paris, where could one go but to Ritz's? Did he see her in some grubby hole across the river? Or in a family *pension* near the Place de l'Etoile? There was no affectation in her tendency to gravitate toward what was costliest and most conspicuous. In doing so she obeyed one of the profoundest instincts of her nature, and it was another instinct which taught her to gratify the first at any cost, even to that of dipping into the pocket of an impecunious newspaper correspondent. It was a part of her strength—and of her charm too—that she did such things naturally, openly, without any of the ugly grimaces of dissimulation or compunction.

Her recourse to Garnett had of course marked a specially low ebb in her fortunes. Save in moments of exceptional dearth she had richer sources of supply; and he was nearly sure that, by running over the "society column" of the Paris *Herald,* he should find an explanation, not perhaps of her presence at Ritz's, but of her means of subsistence there. What really perplexed him was not the financial but the social aspect of the case. When Mrs. Newell had left London in July she had told him that, between Cowes and Scotland, she and Hermy were provided for till the middle of October: after that, as she put it, they would have to look about. Why, then, when she had in her hand the opportunity of living for three months at the expense of the British aristocracy, did she rush off to Paris at heaven knew whose expense in the beginning of September? She was not a woman to act incoherently; if she made mistakes they were not of that kind. Garnett felt sure she would never willingly relax her hold on her distinguished friends—was it possible that it was they who had somewhat violently let go of her?

As Garnett reviewed the situation he began to see that this possibility had for some time been latent in it. He had felt that something might happen at any moment—and was not this the something he had obscurely foreseen? Mrs. Newell really moved too fast: her position was as perilous as that of an invading army without a base of supplies. She used up everything too quickly—friends, credit, influence, forbearance. It was so easy for her to acquire all these—what a pity she had never learned to keep them! He himself, for instance—the most insignificant of her acquisitions—was beginning to feel like a squeezed sponge at the mere thought of her; and it was this sense of exhaustion, of the inability to provide more, either materially or morally, which had provoked his exclamation on opening her note. From the first days of their acquaintance her prodigality had amazed him, but he had believed it to be surpassed by the infinity of her resources. If she exhausted old supplies she always found new ones to replace them. When one set of people began to find her impossible, another was always beginning to find her indispensable. Yes—but there were limits—there were only so many sets of people, at least in her social classification, and when she came to an end of them, what then? Was this flight to Paris a sign that she had come to an end—was she going to try Paris because London had failed her? The time of year precluded such a conjecture. Mrs. Newell's Paris was non-existent in September. The town was a desert of gaping trippers—he could as soon think of her seeking social restoration at Margate.

For a moment it occurred to him that she might have to come over to replenish her wardrobe; but he knew her dates too well to dwell long on this hope. It was in April and December that she visited the dressmakers: before December, he had heard her explain, one got nothing but "the American fashions." Mrs. Newell's scorn of all things American was somewhat illogically coupled with the determination to use her own Americanism to the utmost as a means of social advance. She had found out long ago that, on certain lines, it paid in London to be American, and she had manufactured for herself a personality independent of geographical or social demarcations, and presenting that remarkable blend of plantation dialect, Bowery slang and hyperbolic statement, which is the British nobility's favorite idea of an unadulterated Americanism. Mrs. Newell, for all her talents, was not naturally either humorous or hyperbolic, and there were times when it would doubtless have been a relief to her to be as monumentally stolid as some of the persons whose dulness it was her fate to enliven. It was perhaps the need of relaxing which had drawn her into her odd intimacy with Garnett, with whom she did not have to be either scrupulously English or artificially American, since the impression she made on him was of no more consequence than that which she produced on her footman. Garnett was perfectly aware that he owed his success to his insignificance, but the fact affected him only as adding one more element to his knowledge of Mrs. Newell's character. He was as ready to sacrifice his personal vanity in such a cause as he had been, at the outset of their acquaintance, to sacrifice his professional pride to the opportunity of knowing her.

When he had accepted the position of "London correspondent" (with an occasional side-glance at Paris) to the New York *Searchlight*, he had not understood that his work was to include the obligation of "interviewing"; indeed, had the possibility presented itself in advance, he would have met it by unpacking his valise and returning to the drudgery of his assistant-editorship in New York. But when, after three months in Europe, he received a letter from his chief, suggesting that he should enliven the Sunday *Searchlight* by a series of "Talks with Smart Americans in London" (beginning, say, with Mrs. Sam Newell), the change of focus already enabled him to view the proposal without passion. For his life on the edge of the great world-caldron of art, politics and pleasure—of that high-spiced brew which is nowhere else so subtly and variously compounded—had bred in him an eager appetite to taste of the heady mixture. He knew he should never have the full spoon at his lips, but he recalled the peasant-girl in one of Browning's plays, who has once eaten polenta cut with a knife which has carved an ortolan. Might not Mrs. Newell, who had so successfully cut a way into the dense and succulent mass of English society, serve as the knife to season his polenta?

He had expected, as the result of the interview, to which she promptly, almost eagerly, assented, no more than the glimpse of brightly lit vistas which a waiting messenger may catch through open doors; but instead he had found himself drawn at once into the inner sanctuary, not of London society, but of Mrs. Newell's relation to it. She had been candidly charmed by the idea of the interview: it struck him that she was conscious of the need of being freshened up. Her appearance was brilliantly fresh, with the inveterate freshness of the toilet-table; her paint was as impenetrable as armor. But her personality was a little tarnished: she was in want of social renovation. She had been doing and saying the same things for too long a time. London, Cowes, Homburg, Scotland, Monte Carlo—that had been the round since Hermy was a baby. Hermy was her daughter, Miss Hermione Newell, who was called in presently to be shown off to the interviewer and add a paragraph to the celebration of her mother's charms.

Miss Newell's appearance was so full of an unassisted freshness that for a moment Garnett made the mistake of fancying that she could fill a paragraph of her own. But he soon found that her vague personality was merely tributary to her parent's; that her youth and grace were, in some mysterious way, her mother's rather than her own. She smiled obediently on Garnett, but could contribute little beyond her smile and the general sweetness of her presence, to the picture of Mrs. Newell's existence which it was the young man's business to draw. And presently he found that she had left the room without his noticing it.

He learned in time that this unnoticeableness was the most conspicuous thing about her. Burning at best with a mild light, she became invisible in the glare of her mother's personality. It was in fact only as a product of her environment that poor Hermione struck the imagination. With the smartest woman in London as her guide and example she had never developed a taste for dress, and with opportunities for enlightenment from which Garnett's fancy recoiled she remained simple, unsuspicious and tender, with an inclination to good works and afternoon church, a taste for the society of dull girls, and a clinging fidelity to old governesses and retired nurse-maids. Mrs. Newell, whose boast it was that she looked facts in the face, frankly owned that she had not been able to make anything of Hermione. "If she has a role I haven't discovered it," she confessed to Garnett. "I've tried everything, but she doesn't fit in anywhere."

Mrs. Newell spoke as if her daughter were a piece of furniture acquired without due reflection, and for which no suitable place could be found. She got, of course, what she could out of Hermione, who wrote her notes, ran her errands, saw tiresome people for her, and occupied an intermediate office between that of lady's maid and secretary; but such small returns on her investment were not what Mrs. Newell had counted on. What was the use of producing and educating a handsome daughter if she did not, in some more positive way, contribute to her parent's advancement?

III

"IT's about Hermy," Mrs. Newell said, rising from the heap of embroidered cushions which formed the background of her afternoon repose.

Her sitting-room at Ritz's was full of penetrating warmth and fragrance. Long-stemmed roses filled the vases on the chimney-piece, in which a fire sparkled with that effect of luxury which fires produce when the weather is not cold enough to justify them. On the writing-table, among notes and cards, and signed photographs of celebrities, Mrs. Newell's gold inkstand, her jewelled penholder, her heavily-monogrammed despatch-box, gave back from their expensive surfaces the glint of the flame, which sought out and magnified the orient of the pearls among the lady's laces and found a mirror in the pinky polish of her finger-tips. It was just such a scene as a little September fire, lit for show and not for warmth, would delight to dwell on and pick out in all its opulent details; and even Garnett, inured to Mrs. Newell's capacity for extracting manna from the desert, reflected that she must have found new fields to glean.

"It's about Hermy," she repeated, making room for him among the cushions. "I had to see you at once. We came over yesterday from London."

Garnett, seating himself, continued his leisurely survey of the room. In the glitter of Mrs. Newell's magnificence Hermione, as usual, faded out of sight, and he hardly noticed her mother's allusion.

"I have never seen you more resplendent," he remarked.

She received the tribute with complacency. "The rooms are not bad, are they? We came over with the Woolsey Hubbards (you've heard of them, of course?—they're from Detroit), and really they do things very decently. Their motor-car met us at Boulogne, and the courier always wires ahead to have the rooms filled with flowers. This *salon*, is really a part of their suite. I simply couldn't have afforded it myself."

She delivered these facts in a high decisive voice, which had a note akin to the clink of her many bracelets and the rattle of her ringed hands against the enamelled cigarette-case which she extended to Garnett after helping herself from its contents.

"You are always meeting such charming people," said Garnett with mild irony; and, reverting to her first remark, he bethought himself to add: "I hope Miss Hermione is not ill?"

"Ill? She was never ill in her life," exclaimed Mrs. Newell, as though her daughter had been accused of an indelicacy.

"It was only that you said you had come over on her account."

"So I have. Hermione is to be married."

Mrs. Newell brought out the words impressively, drawing back to observe their effect on her visitor. It was such that he received them with a long silent stare, which finally passed into a cry of wonder. "Married? For heaven's sake, to whom?"

Mrs. Newell continued to regard him with a smile so serene and victorious that he saw she took his somewhat unseemly astonishment as a merited tribute to her genius. Presently she extended a glittering hand and took a sheet of note paper from the blotter.

"You can have that put in to-morrow's *Herald*," she said.

Garnett, receiving the paper, read in Hermione's own finished hand: "A marriage has been arranged, and will shortly take place, between the Comte Louis du Trayas, son of the Marquis du Trayas de la Baume, and Miss Hermione Newell, daughter of Samuel C. Newell Esqre. of Elmira, N. Y. Comte Louis du Trayas belongs to one of the oldest and most distinguished families in France, and is equally well connected in England, being the nephew of Lord Saint Priscoe and a cousin of the Countess of Morningfield, whom he frequently visits at Adham and Portlow."

The perusal of this document filled Garnett with such deepening wonder that he could not, for the moment, even do justice to the strangeness of its being written out for publication in the bride's own hand. Hermione a bride! Hermione a future countess! Hermione on the brink of a marriage which would give her not only a great "situation" in the Parisian world but a footing in some of the best houses in England! Regardless of its unflattering implications, Garnett prolonged his stare of mute amazement till Mrs. Newell somewhat sharply exclaimed—"Well, didn't I always tell you that she would marry a Frenchman?"

Garnett, in spite of himself, smiled at this revised version of his hostess's frequent assertion that Hermione was too goody-goody to take in England, but that with her little dowdy air she might very well "go off" in the Faubourg if only a *dot* could be raked up for her—and the recollection flashed a new light on the versatility of Mrs. Newell's genius.

"But how did you do it—?" was on the tip of his tongue; and he had barely time to give the query the more conventional turn of: "How did it happen?"

"Oh, we were up at Glaish with the Edmund Fitzarthurs. Lady Edmund is a sort of cousin of the Morningfields', who have a shooting-lodge near Glaish—a place called Portlow—and young Trayas was there with them. Lady Edmund, who is a dear, drove Hermy over to Portlow, and the thing was done in no time. He simply fell over head and ears in love with her. You know Hermy is really very handsome in her peculiar way. I don't think you have ever appreciated her," Mrs. Newell summed up with a note of exquisite reproach.

"I've appreciated her, I assure you; but one somehow didn't think of her marrying—so soon."

"Soon? She's three-and-twenty; but you've no imagination," said Mrs. Newell; and Garnett inwardly admitted that he had not enough to soar to the heights of her invention. For the marriage, of course, was an invention of her own, a superlative stroke of business, in which he was sure the principal parties had all been passive agents, in which everyone, from the bankrupt and disreputable Fitzarthurs to the rich and immaculate Morningfields, had by some mysterious sleight of hand been made to fit into Mrs. Newell's designs. But it was not enough for Garnett to marvel at her work—he wanted to understand it, to take it apart, to find out how the trick had been done. It was true that Mrs. Newell had always said Hermy might go off in the Faubourg if she had a *dot*—but even Mrs. Newell's juggling could hardly conjure up a *dot:* such feats as she was able to perform in this line were usually made to serve her own urgent necessities. And besides, who was likely to take sufficient interest in Hermione to supply her with the means of marrying a French nobleman? The flowers ordered in advance by the Woolsey Hubbards' courier made Garnett wonder if that accomplished functionary had also wired over to have Miss Newell's settlements drawn up. But of all the comments hovering on his lips the only one he could decently formulate was the remark that he supposed Mrs. Newell and her daughter had come over to see the young man's family and make the final arrangements.

"Oh, they're made—everything is settled," said Mrs. Newell, looking him squarely in the eye. "You're wondering, of course, about the *dot*—Frenchmen never go off their heads to the extent of forgetting *that;* or at least their parents don't allow them to."

Garnett murmured a vague assent, and she went on without the least appearance of resenting his curiosity: "It all came about so fortunately. Only fancy, just the week they met I got a little legacy from an aunt in Elmira—a good soul I hadn't seen or heard of for years. I suppose I ought to have put on mourning for her, by the way, but it would have eaten up a good bit of the legacy, and I really needed it all for poor Hermy. Oh, it's not a fortune, you understand—but the young man is madly in love, and has always had his own way, so after a lot of correspondence it's been arranged. They saw Hermy this morning, and they're enchanted."

"And the marriage takes place very soon?"

"Yes, in a few weeks, here. His mother is an invalid and couldn't have gone to England. Besides, the French don't travel. And as Hermy has become a Catholic—"

"Already?"

Mrs. Newell stared. "It doesn't take long. And it suits Hermy exactly—she can go to church so much oftener. So I thought," Mrs. Newell concluded with dignity, "that a wedding at Saint Philippe du Roule would be the most suitable thing at this season."

"Dear me," said Garnett, "I am left breathless—I can't catch up with you. I suppose even the day is fixed, though Miss Hermione doesn't mention it," and he indicated the official announcement in his hand.

Mrs. Newell laughed. "Hermy had to write that herself, poor dear, because my scrawl's too hideous—but I dictated it. No, the day isn't fixed—that's why I sent for you." There was a splendid directness about Mrs. Newell. It would never have occurred to her to pretend to Garnett that she had summoned him for the pleasure of his company.

"You've sent for me—to fix the day?" he enquired humourously.

"To remove the last obstacle to its being fixed."

"I? What kind of an obstacle could I have the least effect on?"

Mrs. Newell met his banter with a look which quelled it. "I want you to find her father."

"Her father? Miss Hermione's—?"

"My husband, of course. I suppose you know he's living."

Garnett blushed at his own clumsiness. "I—yes—that is, I really knew nothing—" he stammered, feeling that each word added to it. If Hermione was unnoticeable, Mr. Newell had always been invisible. The young man had never so much as given him a thought, and it was awkward to come on him so suddenly at a turn of the talk.

"Well, he is—living here in Paris," said Mrs. Newell, with a note of asperity which seemed to imply that her friend might have taken the trouble to post himself on this point.

"In Paris? But in that case isn't it quite simple—?"

"To find him? I daresay it won't be difficult, though he is rather mysterious. But the point is that I can't go to him—and that if I write to him he won't answer."

"Ah," said Garnett thoughtfully.

"And so you've got to find him for me, and tell him."

"Tell him what?"

"That he must come to the wedding—that we must show ourselves together at church and at the breakfast."

She delivered the behest in her sharp imperative key, the tone of the born commander. But for once Garnett ventured to question her orders.

"And supposing he won't come?"

"He must if he cares for his daughter's happiness. She can't be married without him."

"Can't be married?"

"The French are like that—especially the old families. I was given to understand at once that my husband must appear—if only to establish the fact that we're not divorced."

"Ah—you're *not*, then?" escaped from Garnett.

"Mercy, no! Divorce is stupid. They don't like it in Europe. And in this case it would have been the end of Hermy's marriage. They wouldn't think of letting their son marry the child of divorced parents."

"How fortunate, then—"

"Yes; but I always think of such things beforehand. And of course I've told them that my husband will be present."

"You think he will consent?"

"No; not at first; but you must make him. You must tell him how sweet Hermione is—and you must see Louis, and be able to describe their happiness. You must dine here to-night—he is coming. We're all dining with the Hubbards, and they expect you. They have given Hermy some very good diamonds—though I should have preferred a cheque, as she'll be horribly poor. But I think Kate Hubbard means to do something about the trousseau—Hermy is at Paquin's with her now. You've no idea how delightful all our friends have been.—Ah, here is one of them now," she broke off smiling, as the door opened to admit, without preliminary announcement, a gentleman so glossy and ancient, with such a fixed unnatural freshness of smile and eye, that he gave Garnett the effect of having been embalmed and then enamelled. It needed not the exotic-looking ribbon in the visitor's button-hole, nor Mrs. Newell's introduction of him as her friend Baron Schenkelderff, to assure Garnett of his connection with a race as ancient as his appearance.

Baron Schenkelderff greeted his hostess with paternal playfulness, and the young man with an ease which might have been acquired on the Stock Exchange and in the dressing-rooms of "leading ladies." He spoke a faultless, colourless English, from which one felt he might pass with equal mastery to half a dozen other languages. He enquired patronizingly for the excellent Hubbards, asked his hostess if she did not mean to give him a drop of tea and a cigarette, remarked that he need not ask if Hermione was still closeted with the dress-maker, and, on the waiter's coming in answer to his ring, ordered the tea himself, and added a request for *fine champagne*. It was not the first time that Garnett had seen such minor liberties taken in Mrs. Newell's drawing-room, but they had hitherto been taken by persons who had at least the superiority of knowing what they were permitting themselves, whereas the young man felt almost sure that Baron Schenkelderff's manner was the most distinguished he could achieve; and this deepened the disgust with which, as the minutes passed, he yielded to the conviction that the Baron was Mrs. Newell's aunt.

IV

GARNETT had always foreseen that Mrs. Newell might some day ask him to do something he should greatly dislike. He had never gone so far as to conjecture what it might be, but had simply felt that if he allowed his acquaintance with her to pass from spectatorship to participation he must be prepared to find himself, at any moment, in a queer situation.

The moment had come; and he was relieved to find that he could meet it by refusing her request. He had not always been sure that she would leave him this alternative. She had a way of involving people in her complications without their being aware of it, and Garnett had pictured himself in holes so tight that there might not be room for a wriggle. Happily in this case he could still move freely. Nothing compelled him to act as an intermediary between Mrs. Newell and her husband, and it was preposterous to suppose that, even in a life of such perpetual upheaval as hers, there were no roots which struck deeper than her casual intimacy with himself. She had simply laid hands on him because he happened to be within reach, and he would put himself out of reach by leaving for London on the morrow.

Having thus inwardly asserted his independence, he felt free to let his fancy dwell on the strangeness of the situation. He had always supposed that Mrs. Newell, in her flight through life, must have thrown a good many victims to the wolves, and had assumed that Mr. Newell had been among the number. That he had been dropped overboard at an early stage in the lady's career seemed probable from the fact that neither his wife nor his daughter ever mentioned him. Mrs. Newell was incapable of reticence, and if her husband had still been an active element in her life he would certainly have figured in her conversation. Garnett, if he thought of the matter at all, had concluded that divorce must long since have eliminated Mr. Newell; but he now saw how he had underrated his friend's faculty for using up the waste material of life. She had always struck him as the most extravagant of women, yet it turned out that by a miracle of thrift she had for years kept a superfluous husband on the chance that he might some day be useful to her. The day had come, and Mr. Newell was to be called from his obscurity. Garnett wondered what had become of him in the interval, and in what shape he would respond to the evocation. The fact that his wife feared he might not respond to it at all, seemed to show that his exile was voluntary, or had at least come to appear preferable to other alternatives; but if that were the case it was curious that he should not have taken legal means to free himself. He could hardly have had his wife's motives for wishing to maintain the vague tie between them; but conjecture lost itself in trying to picture what his point of view was likely to be, and Garnett, on his way to the Hubbards' dinner that evening, could not help regretting that circumstances denied him the opportunity of meeting so enigmatic a person. The young man's knowledge of Mrs. Newell's methods made him feel that her husband might be an interesting study. This, however, did not affect his resolve to keep clear of the business. He entered the Hubbards' dining-room with the firm intention of refusing to execute Mrs. Newell's commission, and if he changed his mind in the course of the evening it was not owing to that lady's persuasions.

Garnett's curiosity as to the Hubbards' share in Hermione's marriage was appeased before he had been seated five minutes at their table.

Mrs. Woolsey Hubbard was an expansive blonde, whose ample but disciplined outline seemed the result of a well-matched struggle between her cook and her corset-maker. She talked a great deal of what was appropriate in dress and conduct, and seemed to regard Mrs. Newell as a final arbiter on both points. To do or to wear anything inappropriate would have been extremely mortifying to Mrs. Hubbard, and she was evidently resolved, at the price of eternal vigilance, to prove her familiarity with what she frequently referred to as "the right thing." Mr. Hubbard appeared to have no such preoccupations. Garnett, if called upon to describe him, would have done so by saying that he was the American who always pays. The young man, in the course of his foreign wanderings, had come across many fellow-citizens of Mr. Hubbard's type, in the most diverse company and surroundings; and wherever they were to be found, they always had their hands in their pockets. Mr. Hubbard's standard of gentility was the extent of a man's capacity to "foot the bill"; and as no one but an occasional compatriot cared to dispute the privilege with him, he seldom had reason to doubt his social superiority.

Garnett, nevertheless, did not believe that this lavish pair were, as Mrs. Newell would have phrased it, "putting up" Hermione's *dot*. They would go very far in diamonds, but they would hang back from securities. Their readiness to pay was indefinably mingled with a dread of being expected to, and their prodigalities would take flight at the first hint of coercion. Mrs. Newell, who had had a good deal of experience in managing this type of millionaire, could be trusted not to arouse their susceptibilities, and Garnett was therefore certain that the chimerical legacy had been extracted from other pockets. There were none in view but those of Baron Schenkelderff, who, seated at Mrs. Hubbard's right, with a new order in his button-hole, and a fresh glaze upon his features, enchanted that lady by his careless references to crowned heads and his condescending approval of the champagne. Garnett was more than ever certain that it was the Baron who was paying; and it was this conviction which made him suddenly feel that, at any cost, Hermione's marriage must take place. He had felt no special interest in the marriage except as one more proof of Mrs. Newell's extraordinary capacity; but now it appealed to him from the girl's own stand-point. For he saw, with a touch of compunction, that in the mephitic air of her surroundings a love-story of surprising freshness had miraculously flowered. He had only to intercept the glances which the young couple exchanged to find himself transported to the candid region of romance. It was evident that Hermione adored and was adored; that the lovers believed in each other and in every one about them, and that even the legacy of the defunct aunt had not been too great a strain on their faith in human nature.

His first glance at the Comte Louis du Trayas showed Garnett that, by some marvel of fitness, Hermione had happened upon a kindred nature. If the young man's long mild features and short-sighted glance revealed no special force of character, they showed a benevolence and simplicity as incorruptible as her own, and declared that their possessor, whatever his failings, would never imperil the illusions she had so miraculously preserved. The fact that the girl took her good fortune naturally, and did not regard herself as suddenly snatched from the jaws of death, added poignancy to the situation; for if she missed this way of escape, and was thrown back on her former life, the day of discovery could not be long deferred. It made Garnett shiver to think of her growing old between her mother and Schenkelderff, or such successors of the Baron's as might probably attend on Mrs. Newell's waning fortunes; for it was clear to him that the Baron marked the first stage in his friend's decline. When Garnett took leave that evening he had promised Mrs. Newell that he would try to find her husband.

V

IF Mr. Newell read in the papers the announcement of his daughter's marriage it did not cause him to lift the veil of seclusion in which his wife represented him as shrouded.

A round of the American banks in Paris failed to give Garnett his address, and it was only in chance talk with one of the young secretaries of the Embassy that he was put on Mr. Newell's track. The secretary's father, it appeared, had known the Newells some twenty years earlier. He had had business relations with Mr. Newell, who was then a man of property, with factories or something of the kind, the narrator thought, somewhere in Western New York. There had been at this period, for Mrs. Newell, a phase of large hospitality and showy carriages in Washington and at Narragansett. Then her husband had had reverses, had lost heavily in Wall Street, and had finally drifted abroad and been lost to sight. The young man did not know at what point in his financial decline Mr. Newell had parted company with his wife and daughter; "though you may bet your hat," he philosophically concluded, "that the old girl hung on as long as there were any pickings." He did not himself know Mr. Newell's address, but opined that it might be extracted from a certain official at the Consulate, if Garnett could give a sufficiently good reason for the request; and here in fact Mrs. Newell's emissary learned that her husband was to be found in an obscure street of the Luxembourg quarter.

In order to be near the scene of action, Garnett went to breakfast at his usual haunt, determined to despatch his business as early in the day as politeness allowed. The head waiter welcomed him to a table near that of the transatlantic sage, who sat in his customary corner, his head tilted back against the blistered mirror at an angle suggesting that in a freer civilization his feet would have sought the same level. He greeted Garnett affably and the two exchanged their usual generalizations on life till the sage rose to go; whereupon it occurred to Garnett to accompany him. His friend took the offer in good part, merely remarking that he was going to the Luxembourg gardens, where it was his invariable habit, on good days, to feed the sparrows with the remains of his breakfast roll; and Garnett replied that, as it happened, his own business lay in the same direction.

"Perhaps, by the way," he added, "you can tell me how to find the rue Panonceaux where I must go presently. I thought I knew this quarter fairly well, but I have never heard of it."

His companion came to a sudden halt on the narrow sidewalk, to the confusion of the dense and desultory traffic which marks the old streets of the Latin quarter. He fixed his mild eye on Garnett and gave a twist to the cigar which lingered in the corner of his mouth.

"The rue Panonceaux? It *is* an out of the way hole, but I can tell you how to find it," he answered.

He made no motion to do so, however, but continued to bend on the young man the full force of his interrogative gaze; then he added abruptly: "Would you mind telling me your object in going there?"

Garnett looked at him with surprise: a question so unblushingly personal was strangely out of keeping with his friend's usual attitude of detachment. Before he could reply, however, the other had quietly continued: "Do you happen to be in search of Samuel C. Newell?"

"Why, yes, I am," said Garnett with a start of conjecture.

His companion uttered a sigh. "I supposed so," he said resignedly; "and in that case," he added, "we may as well have the matter out in the Luxembourg."

Garnett had halted before him with deepening astonishment. "But you don't mean to tell me—?" he stammered.

The little man made a motion of assent. "I am Samuel C. Newell," he said drily; "and if you have no objection, I prefer not to break through my habit of feeding the sparrows. We are five minutes late as it is."

He quickened his pace without awaiting any reply from Garnett, who walked beside him in unsubdued wonder till they reached the Luxembourg gardens, where Mr. Newell, making for one of the less frequented alleys, seated himself on a bench and drew the fragment of a roll from his pocket. His coming was evidently expected, for a shower of little dusky bodies at once descended on him, and the gravel fluttered with battling wings and beaks as he distributed his dole with impartial gestures.

It was not till the ground was white with crumbs, and the first frenzy of his pensioners appeased, that he turned to Garnett and said: "I presume, sir, that you come from my wife."

Garnett coloured with embarrassment: the more simply the old man took his mission the more complicated it appeared to himself.

"From your wife—and from Miss Newell," he said at length. "You have perhaps heard that she is to be married."

"Oh, yes—I read the *Herald* pretty faithfully," said Miss Newell's parent, shaking out another handful of crumbs.

Garnett cleared his throat. "Then you have no doubt thought it natural that, under the circumstances, they should wish to communicate with you."

The sage continued to fix his attention on the sparrows. "My wife," he remarked, "might have written to me."

"Mrs. Newell was afraid she might not hear from you in reply."

"In reply? Why should she? I suppose she merely wishes to announce the marriage. She knows I have no money left to buy wedding-presents," said Mr. Newell astonishingly.

Garnett felt his colour deepen: he had a vague sense of standing as the representative of something guilty and enormous, with which he had rashly identified himself.

"I don't think you understand," he said. "Mrs. Newell and your daughter have asked me to see you because they are anxious that you should consent to appear at the wedding."

Mr. Newell, at this, ceased to give his attention to the birds, and turned a compassionate gaze upon Garnett.

"My dear sir—I don't know your name—" he remarked, "would you mind telling me how long you have been acquainted with Mrs. Newell?" And without waiting for an answer he added judicially: "If you wait long enough she will ask you to do some very disagreeable things for her."

This echo of his own thoughts gave Garnett a sharp twinge of discomfort, but he made shift to answer good-humouredly: "If you refer to my present errand, I must tell you that I don't find it disagreeable to do anything which may be of service to Miss Hermione."

Mr. Newell fumbled in his pocket, as though searching unavailingly for another morsel of bread; then he said: "From her point of view I shall not be the most important person at the ceremony."

Garnett smiled. "That is hardly a reason—" he began; but he was checked by the brevity of tone with which his companion replied: "I am not aware that I am called upon to give you my reasons."

"You are certainly not," the young man rejoined, "except in so far as you are willing to consider me as the messenger of your wife and daughter."

"Oh, I accept your credentials," said the other with his dry smile; "what I don't recognize is their right to send a message."

This reduced Garnett to silence, and after a moment's pause Mr. Newell drew his watch from his pocket.

"I am sorry to cut the conversation short, but my days are mapped out with a certain regularity, and this is the hour for my nap." He rose as he spoke and held out his hand with a glint of melancholy humour in his small clear eyes.

"You dismiss me, then? I am to take back a refusal?" the young man exclaimed.

"My dear sir, those ladies have got on very well without me for a number of years: I imagine they can put through this wedding without my help."

"You are mistaken, then; if it were not for that I shouldn't have undertaken this errand."

Mr. Newell paused as he was turning away. "Not for what?" he enquired.

"The fact that, as it happens, the wedding can't be put through without your help."

Mr. Newell's thin lips formed a noiseless whistle. "They've got to have my consent, have they? Well, is he a good young man?"

"The bridegroom?" Garnett echoed in surprise. "I hear the best accounts of him—and Miss Newell is very much in love."

Her parent met this with an odd smile. "Well, then, I give my consent—it's all I've got left to give," he added philosophically.

Garnett hesitated. "But if you consent—if you approve—why do you refuse your daughter's request?"

Mr. Newell looked at him a moment. "Ask Mrs. Newell!" he said. And as Garnett was again silent, he turned away with a slight gesture of leave-taking.

But in an instant the young man was at his side. "I will not ask your reasons, sir," he said, "but I will give you mine for being here. Miss

Newell cannot be married unless you are present at the ceremony. The young man's parents know that she has a father living, and they give their consent only on condition that he appears at her marriage. I believe it is customary in old French families—."

"Old French families be damned!" said Mr. Newell with sudden vigour. "She had better marry an American." And he made a more decided motion to free himself from Garnett's importunities.

But his resistance only strengthened the young man's. The more unpleasant the latter's task became, the more unwilling he grew to see his efforts end in failure. During the three days which had been consumed in his quest it had become clear to him that the bridegroom's parents, having been surprised into a reluctant consent, were but too ready to withdraw it on the plea of Mr. Newell's non-appearance. Mrs. Newell, on the last edge of tension, had confided to Garnett that the Morningfields were "being nasty"; and he could picture the whole powerful clan, on both sides of the Channel, arrayed in a common resolve to exclude poor Hermione from their ranks. The very inequality of the contest stirred his blood, and made him vow that in this case at least the sins of the parents should not be visited on the children. In his talk with the young secretary he had obtained some glimpses of Baron Schenkelderff's past which fortified this resolve. The Baron, at one time a familiar figure in a much-observed London set, had been mixed up in an ugly money-lending business ending in suicide, which had excluded him from the society most accessible to his race. His alliance with Mrs. Newell was doubtless a desperate attempt at rehabilitation, a forlorn hope on both sides, but likely to be an enduring tie because it represented, to both partners, their last chance of escape from social extinction. That Hermione's marriage was a mere stake in their game did not in the least affect Garnett's view of its urgency. If on their part it was a sordid speculation, to her it had the freshness of the first wooing. If it made of her a mere pawn in their hands, it would put her, so Garnett hoped, beyond farther risk of such base uses; and to achieve this had become a necessity to him.

The sense that, if he lost sight of Mr. Newell, the latter might not easily be found again, nerved Garnett to hold his ground in spite of the resistance he encountered; and he tried to put the full force of his plea into the tone with which he cried: "Ah, you don't know your daughter!"

VI

MRS. NEWELL, that afternoon, met him on the threshold of her sitting-room with a "Well?" of pent-up anxiety.

In the room itself, Baron Schenkelderff sat with crossed legs and head thrown back, in an attitude which he did not see fit to alter at the young man's approach.

Garnett hesitated; but it was not the summariness of the Baron's greeting which he resented.

"You've found him?" Mrs. Newell exclaimed.

"Yes; but—"

She followed his glance and answered it with a slight shrug. "I can't take you into my room, because there's a dress-maker there, and she won't go because she is waiting to be paid. Schenkelderff," she exclaimed, "you're not wanted; please go and look out of the window."

The Baron rose and, lighting a cigarette, laughingly retired to the embrasure. Mrs. Newell flung herself down and signed to Garnett to take a seat at her side.

"Well—you've found him? You've talked with him?"

"Yes; I have talked with him—for an hour."

She made an impatient movement. "That's too long! Does he refuse?"

"He doesn't consent."

"Then you mean—?"

"He wants time to think it over."

"Time? There *is* no time—did you tell him so?"

"I told him so; but you must remember that he has plenty. He has taken twenty-four hours."

Mrs. Newell groaned. "Oh, that's too much. When he thinks things over he always refuses."

"Well, he would have refused at once if I had not agreed to the delay."

She rose nervously from her seat and pressed her hands to her forehead. "It's too hard, after all I've done! The trousseau is ordered—think how disgraceful! You must have managed him badly; I'll go and see him myself."

The Baron, at this, turned abruptly from his study of the Place Vendome.

"My dear creature, for heaven's sake don't spoil everything!" he exclaimed.

Mrs. Newell coloured furiously. "What's the meaning of that brilliant speech?"

"I was merely putting myself in the place of a man on whom you have ceased to smile."

He picked up his hat and stick, nodded knowingly to Garnett, and walked toward the door with an air of creaking jauntiness.

But on the threshold Mrs. Newell waylaid him.

"Don't go—I must speak to you," she said, following him into the antechamber; and Garnett remembered the dress-maker who was not to be dislodged from her bedroom.

In a moment Mrs. Newell returned, with a small flat packet which she vainly sought to dissemble in an inaccessible pocket.

"He makes everything too odious!" she exclaimed; but whether she referred to her husband or the Baron it was left to Garnett to decide.

She sat silent, nervously twisting her cigarette-case between her fingers, while her visitor rehearsed the details of his conversation with Mr. Newell. He did not indeed tell her the arguments he had used to shake her husband's resolve, since in his eloquent sketch of Hermione's situation there had perforce entered hints unflattering to her mother; but he gave the impression that his hearer had in the end been moved, and for that reason had consented to defer his refusal.

"Ah, it's not that—it's to prolong our misery!" Mrs. Newell exclaimed; and after a moment she added drearily: "He has been waiting for such an opportunity for years."

It seemed needless for Garnett to protract his visit, and he took leave with the promise to report at once the result of his final talk with Mr. Newell. But as he was passing through the ante-chamber a side-door opened and Hermione stood before him. Her face was flushed and shaken out of its usual repose of line, and he saw at once that she had been waiting for him.

"Mr. Garnett!" she said in a whisper.

He paused, considering her with surprise: he had never supposed her capable of such emotion as her voice and eyes revealed.

"I want to speak to you; we are quite safe here. Mamma is with the dress-maker," she explained, closing the door behind her, while Garnett laid aside his hat and stick.

"I am at your service," he said.

"You have seen my father? Mamma told me that you were to see him to-day," the girl went on, standing close to him in order that she might not have to raise her voice.

"Yes; I have seen him," Garnett replied with increasing wonder. Hermione had never before mentioned her father to him, and it was by a slight stretch of veracity that he had included her name in her mother's plea to Mr. Newell. He had supposed her to be either unconscious of the transaction, or else too much engrossed in her own happiness to give it a thought; and he had forgiven her the last alternative in consideration of the abnormal character of her filial relations. But now he saw that he must readjust his view of her.

"You went to ask him to come to my wedding; I know about it," Hermione continued. "Of course it is the custom—people will think it odd if he does not come." She paused, and then asked: "Does he consent?"

"No; he has not yet consented."

"Ah, I thought so when I saw Mamma just now!"

"But he hasn't quite refused—he has promised to think it over."

"But he hated it—he hated the idea?"

Garnett hesitated. "It seemed to arouse painful associations."

"Ah, it would—it would!" she exclaimed.

He was astonished at the passion of her accent; astonished still more at the tone with which she went on, laying her hand on his arm: "Mr. Garnett, he must not be asked—he has been asked too often to do things that he hated!"

Garnett looked at the girl with a shock of awe. What abysses of knowledge did her purity hide?

"But, my dear Miss Hermione—" he began.

"I know what you are going to say," she interrupted him. "It is necessary that he should be present at the marriage or the du Trayas will break it off. They don't want it very much, at any rate," she added with a strange candour, "and they will not be sorry, perhaps—for of course Louis would have to obey them."

"So I explained to your father," Garnett assured her.

"Yes—yes; I knew you would put it to him. But that makes no difference, Mr. Garnett. He must not be forced to come unwillingly."

"But if he sees the point—after all, no one can force him!"

"No; but if it is painful to him—if it reminds him too much . . . Oh, Mr. Garnett, I was not a child when he left us. . . . I was old enough to see . . . to see how it must hurt him even now to be reminded. Peace was all he asked for, and I want him to be left in peace!"

Garnett paused in deep embarrassment. "My dear child, there is no need to remind you that your own future—"

She had a gesture that recalled her mother. "My future must take care of itself; he must not be made to see us!" she said imperatively. And as Garnett remained silent she went on: "I have always hoped he did not hate me, but he would hate me now if he were forced to see me."

"Not if he could see you at this moment!" he exclaimed.

She lifted her face with swimming eyes.

"Well, go to him, then; tell him what I have said to you!"

Garnett continued to stand before her, deeply struck. "It might be the best thing," he reflected inwardly; but he did not give utterance to the thought. He merely put out his hand, holding Hermione's in a long pressure.

"I will do whatever you wish," he replied.

"You understand that I am in earnest?" she urged tenaciously.

"I am quite sure of it."

"Then I want you to repeat to him what I have said—I want him to be left undisturbed. I don't want him ever to hear of us again!"

The next day, at the appointed hour, Garnett resorted to the Luxembourg gardens, which Mr. Newell had named as a meeting-place in preference to his own lodgings. It was clear that he did not wish to admit the young man any further into his privacy than the occasion required, and the extreme shabbiness of his dress hinted that pride might be the cause of his reluctance.

Garnett found him feeding the sparrows, but he desisted at the young man's approach, and said at once: "You will not thank me for bringing you all this distance."

"If that means that you are going to send me away with a refusal, I have come to spare you the necessity," Garnett answered.

Mr. Newell turned on him a glance of undisguised wonder, in which an undertone of disappointment might almost have been detected.

"Ah—they've got no use for me, after all?" be said ironically.

Garnett, in reply, related without comment his conversation with Hermione, and the message with which she had charged him. He remembered her words exactly and repeated them without modification, heedless of what they implied or revealed.

Mr. Newell listened with an immovable face, occasionally casting a crumb to his flock. When Garnett ended he asked: "Does her mother know of this?"

" Assuredly not!" cried Garnett with a movement of disgust.

"You must pardon me; but Mrs. Newell is a very ingenious woman." Mr. Newell shook out his remaining crumbs and turned thoughtfully toward Garnett.

"You believe it's quite clear to Hermione that these people will use my refusal as a pretext for backing out of the marriage?"

"Perfectly clear—she told me so herself."

"Doesn't she consider the young man rather chicken-hearted?"

"No; he has already put up a big fight for her, and you know the French look at these things differently. He's only twenty-three and his marrying against his parents' approval is in itself an act of heroism."

"Yes; I believe they look at it that way," Mr. Newell assented. He rose and picked up the half-smoked cigar which he had laid on the bench beside him.

"What do they wear at these French weddings, anyhow? A dress-suit, isn't it?" he asked.

The question was such a surprise to Garnett that for the moment he could only stammer out—"You consent then? I may go and tell her?"

"You may tell my girl—yes." He gave a vague laugh and added: "One way or another, my wife always gets what she wants."

VII

MR. NEWELL'S consent brought with it no accompanying concessions. In the first flush of his success Garnett had pictured himself as bringing together the father and daughter, and hovering in an attitude of benediction over a family group in which Mrs. Newell did not very distinctly figure.

But Mr. Newell's conditions were inflexible. He would "see the thing through" for his daughter's sake; but he stipulated that in the meantime there should be no meetings or farther communications of any kind. He agreed to be ready when Garnett called for him, at the appointed hour on the wedding-day; but until then he begged to be left alone. To this decision he adhered immovably, and when Garnett conveyed it to Hermione she accepted it with a deep look of understanding. As for Mrs. Newell she was too much engrossed in the nuptial preparations to give her husband another thought. She had gained her point, she had disarmed her foes, and in the first flush of success she had no time to remember by what means her victory had been won. Even Garnett's services received little recognition, unless he found them sufficiently compensated by the new look in Hermione's eyes.

The principal figures in Mrs. Newell's foreground were the Woolsey Hubbards and Baron Schenkelderff. With these she was in hourly consultation, and Mrs. Hubbard went about aureoled with the importance of her close connection with an "aristocratic marriage," and dazzled by the Baron's familiarity with the intricacies of the Almanach de Gotha. In his society and Mrs. Newell's, Mrs. Hubbard evidently felt that she had penetrated to the sacred precincts where "the right thing" flourished in its native soil. As for Hermione, her look of happiness had returned, but with an undertint of melancholy, visible perhaps only to Garnett, but to him always hauntingly present. Outwardly she sank back into her passive self, resigned to serve as the brilliant lay-figure on which Mrs. Newell hung the trophies of conquest. Preparations for the wedding were zealously pressed. Mrs. Newell knew the danger of giving people time to think things over, and her fears about her husband being allayed, she began to [87] dread a new attempt at evasion on the part of the bridegroom's family.

"The sooner it's over the sounder I shall sleep!" she declared to Garnett; and all the mitigations of art could not conceal the fact that she was desperately in need of that restorative. There were moments, indeed, when he was sorrier for her than for her husband or her daughter; so black and unfathomable appeared the abyss into which she must slip back if she lost her hold on this last spar of safety.

But she did not lose her hold; his own experience, as well as her husband's declaration, might have told him that she always got what she wanted. How much she had wanted this particular thing was shown by the way in which, on the last day, when all peril was over, she bloomed out in renovated splendour. It gave Garnett a shivering sense of the ugliness of the alternative which had confronted her.

The day came; the showy coupe provided by Mrs. Newell presented itself punctually at Garnett's door, and the young man entered it and drove to the rue Panonceaus. It was a little melancholy back street, with lean old houses sweating rust and damp, and glimpses of pit-life gardens, black and sunless, between walls bristling with iron spikes. On the narrow pavement a blind man pottered along led by a red-eyed poodle: a little farther on a dishevelled woman sat grinding coffee on the threshold of a *buvette*. The bridal carriage stopped before one of the doorways, with a clatter of hoofs and harness which drew the neighbourhood to its windows, and Garnett started to mount the ill-smelling stairs to the fourth floor, on which he learned from the *concierge* that Mr. Newell lodged. But half-way up he met the latter descending, and they turned and went down together.

Hermione's parent wore his usual imperturbable look, and his eye seemed as full as ever of generalisations on human folly; but there was something oddly shrunken and submerged in his appearance, as though he had grown smaller or his clothes larger. And on the last hypothesis Garnett paused—for it became evident to him that Mr. Newell had hired his dress-suit.

Seated at the young man's side on the satin cushions, he remained silent while the carriage rolled smoothly and rapidly through the network of streets leading to the Boulevard Saint-Germain; only once he remarked, glancing at the elaborate fittings of the coupe: "Is this Mrs. Newell's carriage?"

"I believe so—yes," Garnett assented, with the guilty sense that in defining that lady's possessions it was impossible not to trespass on those of her friends.

Mr. Newell made no farther comment, but presently requested his companion to rehearse to him once more the exact duties which were to devolve on him during the coming ceremony. Having mastered these he remained silent, fixing a dry speculative eye on the panorama of the brilliant streets, till the carriage drew up at the entrance of Saint Philippe du Roule.

With the same air of composure he followed his guide through the mob of spectators, and up the crimson velvet steps, at the head of which, but for a word from Garnett, a formidable Suisse, glittering with cocked hat and mace, would have checked the advance of the small crumpled figure so oddly out of keeping with the magnificence of the bridal party. The French fashion prescribing that the family *cortege* shall follow the bride to the altar, the vestibule of the church was thronged with the participatore in the coming procession; but if Mr. Newell felt any nervousness at his sudden projection into this unfamiliar group, nothing in his look or manner betrayed it. He stood beside Garnett till a white-favoured carriage, dashing up to the church with a superlative glitter of highly groomed horseflesh and silver-plated harness, deposited the snowy apparition of the bride, supported by her mother; then, as Hermione entered the vestibule, he went forward quietly to meet her.

The girl, wrapped in the haze of her bridal veil, and a little confused, perhaps, by the anticipation of the meeting, paused a moment, as if in doubt, before the small oddly-clad figure which blocked her path—a horrible moment to Garnett, who felt a pang of misery at this satire on the infallibility of the filial instinct. He longed to make some sign, to break in some way the pause of uncertainty; but before he could move he saw Mrs. Newell give her daughter a sharp push, he saw a blush of compunction flood Hermione's face, and the girl, throwing back her veil, bent her tall head and flung her arms about her father.

Mr. Newell emerged unshaken from the embrace: it seemed to have no effect beyond giving an odder twist to his tie. He stood beside his daughter till the church doors were thrown open; then, at a sign from the verger, he gave her his arm, and the strange couple, with the long train of fashion and finery behind them, started on their march to the altar.

Garnett had already slipped into the church and secured a post of vantage which gave him a side-view over the assemblage. The building was thronged—Mrs. Newell had attained her ambition and given Hermione a smart wedding. Garnett's eye travelled curiously from one group to another—from the numerous representatives of the bridegroom's family, all stamped with the same air of somewhat dowdy distinction, the air of having had their thinking done for them for so long that they could no longer perform the act individually, and the heterogeneous company of Mrs. Newell's friends, who presented, on the opposite side of the nave, every variety of individual conviction in dress and conduct. Of the two groups the latter was decidedly the more interesting to Garnett, who observed that it comprised not only such recent acquisitions as the Woolsey Hubbards and the Baron, but also sundry more important figures which of late had faded to the verse of Mrs. Newell's horizon. Hermione's marriage had drawn them back, bad once more made her mother a social entity, had in short already accomplished the object for which it had been planned and executed.

And as he looked about him Garnett saw that all the other actors in the show faded into insignificance beside the dominant figure of Mrs. Newell, became mere marionettes pulled hither and thither by the hidden wires of her intention. One and all they were there to serve her ends and accomplish her purpose: Schenkelderff and the Hubbards to pay for the show, the bride and bridegroom to seal and symbolize her social rehabilitation, Garnett himself as the humble instrument adjusting the different parts of the complicated machinery, and her husband, finally, as the last stake in her game, the last asset on which she could draw to rebuild her fallen fortunes. At the thought Garnett was filled with a deep disgust for what the scene signified, and for his own share in it. He had been her tool and dupe like the others; if he imagined that he was serving Hermione, it was for her mother's ends that he had worked. What right had he to sentimentalise a marriage founded on such base connivances, and how could he have imagined that in so doing he was acting a disinterested part?

While these thoughts were passing through his mind the ceremony had already begun, and the principal personages in the drama were ranged before him in the row of crimson velvet chairs which fills the foreground of a Catholic marriage. Through the glow of lights and the perfumed haze about the altar, Garnett's eyes rested on the central figures of the group, and gradually the others disappeared from his view and his mind. After all, neither Mrs. Newell's schmes nor his own share in them could ever unsanctify hermione's marriage. It was one more testimony to life's indefatigable renewals, to nature's secret of drawing fragrance from corruption; and as his eyes turned from the girl's illuminated presence to the resigned and stoical figure sunk in the adjoining chair, it occured to him that he had perhaps worked better than he knew in placing them, if only for a moment, side by side.

IN TRUST

I

In the good days, just after we all left college, Ned Halidon and I used to listen, laughing and smoking, while Paul Ambrose set forth his plans.

They were immense, these plans, involving, as it sometimes seemed, the ultimate aesthetic redemption of the whole human race; and provisionally restoring the sense of beauty to those unhappy millions of our fellow country-men who, as Ambrose movingly pointed out, now live and die in surroundings of unperceived and unmitigated ugliness.

"I want to bring the poor starved wretches back to their lost inheritance, to the divine past they've thrown away—I want to make 'em hate ugliness so that they'll smash nearly everything in sight," he would passionately exclaim, stretching his arms across the shabby black-walnut writing-table and shaking his thin consumptive fist in the fact of all the accumulated ugliness in the world.

"You might set the example by smashing that table," I once suggested with youthful brutality; and Paul, pulling himself up, cast a surprised glance at me, and then looked slowly about the parental library, in which we sat.

His parents were dead, and he had inherited the house in Seventeenth Street, where his grandfather Ambrose had lived in a setting of black walnut and pier glasses, giving Madeira dinners, and saying to his guests, as they rejoined the ladies across a florid waste of Aubusson carpet: "This, sir, is Dabney's first study for the Niagara—the Grecian Slave in the bay window was executed for me in Rome twenty years ago by my old friend Ezra Stimpson—" by token of which he passed for a Maecenas in the New York of the 'forties,' and a poem had once been published in the Keepsake or the Book of Beauty "On a picture in the possession of Jonathan Ambrose, Esqre."

Since then the house had remained unchanged. Paul's father, a frugal liver and hard-headed manipulator of investments, did not inherit old Jonathan's artistic sensibilities, and was content to live and die in the unmodified black walnut and red rep of his predecessor. It was only in Paul that the grandfather's aesthetic faculty revived, and Mrs. Ambrose used often to say to her husband, as they watched the little pale-browed boy poring over an old number of the *Art Journal:* "Paul will know how to appreciate your father's treasures."

In recognition of these transmitted gifts Paul, on leaving Harvard, was sent to Paris with a tutor, and established in a studio in which nothing was ever done. He could not paint, and recognized the fact early enough to save himself much wasted labor and his friends many painful efforts in dissimulation. But he brought back a touching enthusiasm for the forms of beauty which an old civilization had revealed to him and an apostolic ardour in the cause of their dissemination.

He had paused in his harangue to take in my ill-timed parenthesis, and the color mounted slowly to his thin cheek-bones.

"It *is* an ugly room," he owned, as though he had noticed the library for the first time.

The desk was carved at the angles with the heads of helmeted knights with long black-walnut moustaches. The red cloth top was worn threadbare, and patterned like a map with islands and peninsulas of ink; and in its centre throned a massive bronze inkstand representing a Syrian maiden slumbering by a well beneath a palm-tree.

"The fact is," I said, walking home that evening with Ned Halidon, "old Paul will never do anything, for the simple reason that he's too stingy."

Ned, who was an idealist, shook his handsome head. "It's not that, my dear fellow. He simply doesn't see things when they're too close to him. I'm glad you woke him up to that desk."

The next time I dined with Paul he said, when we entered the library, and I had gently rejected one of his cheap cigars in favour of a superior article of my own: "Look here, I've been looking round for a decent writing-table. I don't care, as a rule, to turn out old things, especially when they've done good service, but I see now that this is too monstrous—"

"For an apostle of beauty to write his evangel on," I agreed, "it *is* a little inappropriate, except as an awful warning."

Paul colored. "Well, but, my dear fellow, I'd no idea how much a table of this kind costs. I find I can't get anything decent—the plainest mahogany—under a hundred and fifty." He hung his head, and pretended not to notice that I was taking out my own cigar.

"Well, what's a hundred and fifty to you?" I rejoined. "You talk as if you had to live on a book-keeper's salary, with a large family to support."

He smiled nervously and twirled the ring on his thin finger. "I know—I know—that's all very well. But for twenty tables that I *don't* buy I can send some fellow abroad and unseal his eyes."

"Oh, hang it, do both!" I exclaimed impatiently; but the writing-table was never bought. The library remained as it was, and so did the contention between Halidon and myself, as to whether this inconsistent acceptance of his surroundings was due, on our friend's part, to a congenital inability to put his hand in his pocket, or to a real unconsciousness of the ugliness that happened to fall inside his point of vision.

"But he owned that the table was ugly," I agreed.

"Yes, but not till you'd called his attention to the fact; and I'll wager he became unconscious of it again as soon as your back was turned."

"Not before he'd had time to look at a lot of others, and make up his mind that he couldn't afford to buy one."

"That was just his excuse. He'd rather be thought mean than insensible to ugliness. But the truth is that he doesn't mind the table and is used to it. He knows his way about the drawers."

"But he could get another with the same number of drawers."

"Too much trouble," argued Halidon.

"Too much money," I persisted.

"Oh, hang it, now, if he were mean would he have founded three travelling scholarships and be planning this big Academy of Arts?"

"Well, he's mean to himself, at any rate."

"Yes; and magnificently, royally generous to all the world besides!" Halidon exclaimed with one of his great flushes of enthusiasm.

But if, on the whole, the last word remained with Halidon, and Ambrose's personal chariness seemed a trifling foible compared to his altruistic breadth of intention, yet neither of us could help observing, as time went on, that the habit of thrift was beginning to impede the execution of his schemes of art-philanthropy. The three travelling scholarships had been founded in the first blaze of his ardour, and before the personal management of his property had awakened in him the sleeping instincts of parsimony. But as his capital accumulated, and problems of investment and considerations of interest began to encroach upon his visionary hours, we saw a gradual arrest in the practical development of his plan.

"For every thousand dollars he talks of spending on his work, I believe he knocks off a cigar, or buys one less newspaper," Halidon grumbled affectionately; "but after all," he went on, with one of the quick revivals of optimism that gave a perpetual freshness to his spirit, "after all, it makes one admire him all the more when one sees such a nature condemned to be at war with the petty inherited instinct of greed."

Still, I could see it was a disappointment to Halidon that the great project of the Academy of Arts should languish on paper long after all its details had been discussed and settled to the satisfaction of the projector, and of the expert advisers he had called in council.

"He's quite right to do nothing in a hurry—to take advice and compare ideas and points of view—to collect and classify his material in advance," Halidon argued, in answer to a taunt of mine about Paul's perpetually reiterated plea that he was still waiting for So-and-so's report; "but now that the plan's mature—and *such* a plan! You'll grant it's magnificent?—I should think he'd burn to see it carried out, instead of pottering over it till his enthusiasm cools and the whole business turns stale on his hands."

That summer Ambrose went to Europe, and spent his holiday in a frugal walking-tour through Brittany. When he came back he seemed refreshed by his respite from business cares and from the interminable revision of his cherished scheme; while contact with the concrete manifestations of beauty had, as usual, renewed his flagging ardour.

"By Jove," he cried, "whenever I indulged my unworthy eyes in a long gaze at one of those big things—picture or church or statue—I kept saying to myself: 'You lucky devil, you, to be able to provide such a sight as that for eyes that can make some good use of it! Isn't it better to give fifty fellows a chance to paint or carve or build, than to be able to daub canvas or punch clay in a corner all by yourself?'"

"Well," I said, when he had worked off his first ebullition, "when is the foundation stone to be laid?"

His excitement dropped. "The foundation stone—?"

"When are you going to touch the electric button that sets the thing going?"

Paul, with his hands in his sagging pockets, began to pace the library hearth-rug—I can see him now, setting his shabby red slippers between its ramified cabbages.

"My dear fellow, there are one or two points to be considered still—one or two new suggestions I picked up over there—"

I sat silent, and he paused before me, flushing to the roots of his thin hair. "You think I've had time enough—that I ought to have put the thing through before this? I suppose you're right; I can see that even Ned Halidon thinks so; and he has always understood my difficulties better than you have."

This insinuation exasperated me. "Ned would have put it through years ago!" I broke out.

Paul pulled at his straggling moustache. "You mean he has more executive capacity? More—no, it's not that; he's not afraid to spend money, and I am!" he suddenly exclaimed.

He had never before alluded to this weakness to either of us, and I sat abashed, suffering from his evident distress. But he remained planted before me, his little legs wide apart, his eyes fixed on mine in an agony of voluntary self-exposure.

"That's my trouble, and I know it. Big sums frighten me—I can't look them in the face. By George, I wish Ned had the carrying out of this scheme—I wish he could spend my money for me!" His face was lit by the reflection of a passing thought. "Do you know, I shouldn't wonder if I dropped out of the running before either of you chaps, and in case I do I've half a mind to leave everything in trust to Halidon, and let him put the job through for me."

"Much better have your own fun with it," I retorted; but he shook his head, saying with a sigh as he turned away: "It's *not* fun to me—that's the worst of it."

Halidon, to whom I could not help repeating our talk, was amused and touched by his friend's thought.

"Heaven knows what will become of the scheme, if Paul doesn't live to carry it out. There are a lot of hungry Ambrose cousins who will make one gulp of his money, and never give a dollar to the work. Jove, it *would* be a fine thing to have the carrying out of such a plan—but he'll do it yet, you'll see he'll do it yet!" cried Ned, his old faith in his friend flaming up again through the wet blanket of fact.

II

PAUL AMBROSE did not die and leave his fortune to Halidon, but the following summer he did something far more unexpected. He went abroad again, and came back married. Now our busy fancy had never seen Paul married. Even Ned recognized the vague unlikelihood of such a metamorphosis.

"He'd stick at the parson's fee—not to mention the best man's scarf-pin. And I should hate," Ned added sentimentally, "to see 'the touch of a woman's hand' desecrate the sublime ugliness of the ancestral home. Think of such a house made 'cozy'!"

But when the news came he would own neither to surprise nor to disappointment.

"Goodbye, poor Academy!" I exclaimed, tossing over the bridegroom's eight-page rhapsody to Halidon, who had received its duplicate by the same post.

"Now, why the deuce do you say that?" he growled. "I never saw such a beast as you are for imputing mean motives."

To defend myself from this accusation I put out my hand and recovered Paul's letter.

"Here: listen to this. 'Studying art in Paris when I met her—"the vision and the faculty divine, but lacking the accomplishment," etc. . . . A little ethereal profile, like one of Piero della Francesca's angels . . . not rich, thank heaven, *but not afraid of money*, and already enamored of my project for fertilizing my sterile millions . . .'"

"Well, why the deuce—?" Ned began again, as though I had convicted myself out of my friend's mouth; and I could only grumble obscurely: "It's all too pat."

He brushed aside my misgivings. "Thank heaven, she can't paint, any how. And now that I think of it, Paul's just the kind of chap who ought to have a dozen children."

"Ah, then indeed: goodbye, poor Academy!" I croaked.

The lady was lovely, of that there could be no doubt; and if Paul now for a time forgot the Academy, his doing so was but a vindication of his sex. Halidon had only a glimpse of the returning couple before he was himself snatched up in one of the chariots of adventure that seemed perpetually waiting at his door. This time he was going to the far East in the train of a "special mission," and his head was humming with new hopes and ardors; but he had time for a last word with me about Ambrose.

"You'll see—you'll see!" he summed up hopefully as we parted; and what I was to see was, of course, the crowning pinnacle of the Academy lifting itself against the horizon of the immediate future.

It was in the nature of things that I should, meanwhile, see less than formerly of the projector of that unrealized structure. Paul had a personal dread of society, but he wished to show his wife to the world, and I was not often a spectator on these occasions. Paul indeed, good fellow, tried to maintain the pretense of an unbroken intercourse, and to this end I was asked to dine now and then; but when I went I found guests of a new type, who, after dinner, talked of sport and stocks, while their host blinked at them silently through the smoke of his cheap cigars.

The first innovation that struck me was a sudden improvement in the quality of the cigars. Was this Daisy's doing? (Mrs. Ambrose was Daisy.) It was hard to tell—she produced her results so noiselessly. With her fair bent head and vague smile, she seemed to watch life flow by without, as yet, trusting anything of her own to its current. But she was watching, at any rate, and anything might come of that. Such modifications as she produced were as yet almost imperceptible to any but the trained observer. I saw that Paul wished her to be well dressed, but also that he suffered her to drive in a hired brougham, and to have her door opened by the raw-boned Celt who had bumped down the dishes on his bachelor table. The drawing-room curtains were renewed, but this change served only to accentuate the enormities of the carpet, and perhaps discouraged Mrs. Ambrose from farther experiments. At any rate, the desecrating touch that Halidon had affected to dread made no other inroads on the serried ugliness of the Ambrose interior.

In the early summer, when Ned returned, the Ambroses had flown to Europe again—and the Academy was still on paper.

"Well, what do you make of her?" the traveller asked, as we sat over our first dinner together.

"Too many things—and they don't hang together. Perhaps she's still in the chrysalis stage."

"Has Paul chucked the scheme altogether?"

"No. He sent for me and we had a talk about it just before he sailed."

"And what impression did you get?"

"That he had waited to send for me *till* just before he sailed."

"Oh, there you go again!" I offered no denial, and after a pause he asked: "Did *she* ever talk to you about it?"

"Yes. Once or twice—in snatches."

"Well—?"

"She thinks it all *too* beautiful. She would like to see beauty put within the reach of everyone."

"And the practical side—?"

"She says she doesn't understand business."

Halidon rose with a shrug. "Very likely you frightened her with your ugly sardonic grin."

"It's not my fault if my smile doesn't add to the sum-total of beauty."

"Well," he said, ignoring me, "next winter we shall see."

But the next winter did not bring Ambrose back. A brief line, written in November from the Italian lakes, told me that he had "a rotten cough," and that the doctors were packing him off to Egypt. Would I see the architects for him, and explain to the trustees? (The Academy already had trustees, and all the rest of its official hierarchy.) And would they all excuse his not writing more than a word? He was really too groggy—but a little warm weather would set him up again, and he would certainly come home in the spring.

He came home in the spring—in the hold of the ship, with his widow several decks above. The funeral services were attended by all the officers of the Academy, and by two of the young fellows who had won the travelling scholarships, and who shed tears of genuine grief when their benefactor was committed to the grave.

After that there was a pause of suspense—and then the newspapers announced that the late Paul Ambrose had left his entire estate to his widow. The board of the Academy dissolved like a summer cloud, and the secretary lighted his pipe for a year with the official paper of the still-born institution.

After a decent lapse of time I called at the house in Seventeenth Street, and found a man attaching a real-estate agent's sign to the window and a van-load of luggage backing away from the door. The caretaker told me that Mrs. Ambrose was sailing the next morning. Not long afterward I saw the library table with the helmeted knights standing before an auctioneer's door in University Place; and I looked with a pang at the familiar ink-stains, in which I had so often traced the geography of Paul's visionary world.

Halidon, who had picked up another job in the Orient, wrote me an elegiac letter on Paul's death, ending with—"And what about the Academy?" and for all answer I sent him a newspaper clipping recording the terms of the will, and another announcing the sale of the house and Mrs. Ambrose's departure for Europe.

Though Ned and I corresponded with tolerable regularity I received no direct answer to this communication till about eighteen months later, when he surprised me by a letter dated from Florence. It began: "Though she tells me you have never understood her—" and when I had reached that point I laid it down and stared out of my office window at the chimney-pots and the dirty snow on the roof.

"Ned Halidon and Paul's wife!" I murmured; and, incongruously enough, my next thought was: "I wish I'd bought the library table that day."

The letter went on with waxing eloquence: "I could not stand the money if it were not that, to her as well as to me, it represents the sacred opportunity of at last giving speech to his inarticulateness . . ."

"Oh, damn it, they're too glib!" I muttered, dashing the letter down; then, controlling my unreasoning resentment, I read on. "You remember, old man, those words of his that you repeated to me three or four years ago: 'I've half a mind to leave my money in trust to Ned'? Well, it *has* come to me in trust—as if in mysterious fulfillment of his thought; and, oh, dear chap—" I dashed the letter down again, and plunged into my work.

III

"WON'T you own yourself a beast, dear boy?" Halidon asked me gently, one afternoon of the following spring.

I had escaped for a six weeks' holiday, and was lying outstretched beside him in a willow chair on the terrace of their villa above Florence.

My eyes turned from the happy vale at our feet to the illuminated face beside me. A little way off, at the other end of the terrace, Mrs. Halidon was bending over a pot of carnations on the balustrade.

"Oh, cheerfully," I assented.

"You see," he continued, glowing, "living here costs us next to nothing, and it was quite *her* idea, our founding that fourth scholarship in memory of Paul."

I had already heard of the fourth scholarship, but I may have betrayed my surprise at the plural pronoun, for the blood rose under Ned's sensitive skin, and he said with an embarrassed laugh: "Ah, she so completely makes me forget that it's not mine too."

"Well, the great thing is that you both think of it chiefly as his."

"Oh, chiefly—altogether. I should be no more than a wretched parasite if I didn't live first of all for that!"

Mrs. Halidon had turned and was advancing toward us with the slow step of leisurely enjoyment. The bud of her beauty had at last unfolded: her vague enigmatical gaze had given way to the clear look of the woman whose hand is on the clue of life.

"*She's* not living for anything but her own happiness," I mused, "and why in heaven's name should she? But Ned—"

"My wife," Halidon continued, his eyes following mine, "my wife feels it too, even more strongly. You know a woman's sensitiveness. She's—there's nothing she wouldn't do for his memory—because—in other ways. . . . You understand," he added, lowering his tone as she drew nearer, "that as soon as the child is born we mean to go home for good, and take up his work—Paul's work."

Mrs. Halidon recovered slowly after the birth of her child: the return to America was deferred for six months, and then again for a whole year. I heard of the Halidons as established first at Biarritz, then in Rome. The second summer Ned wrote me a line from St. Moritz. He said the place agreed so well with his wife—who was still delicate—that they were "thinking of building a house there: a mere cleft in the rocks, to hide our happiness in when it becomes too exuberant"—and the rest of the letter, very properly, was filled with a rhapsody upon his little daughter. He spoke of her as Paula.

The following year the Halidons reappeared in New York, and I heard with surprise that they had taken the Brereton house for the winter.

"Well, why not?" I argued with myself. "After all, the money is hers: as far as I know the will didn't even hint at a restriction. Why should I expect a pretty woman with two children" (for now there was an heir) "to spend her fortune on a visionary scheme that its originator hadn't the heart to carry out?"

"Yes," cried the devil's advocate—"but Ned?"

My first impression of Halidon was that he had thickened—thickened all through. He was heavier, physically, with the ruddiness of good living rather than of hard training; he spoke more deliberately, and had less frequent bursts of subversive enthusiasm. Well, he was a father, a householder—yes, and a capitalist now. It was fitting that his manner should show a sense of these responsibilities. As for Mrs. Halidon, it was evident that the only responsibilities she was conscious of were those of the handsome woman and the accomplished hostess. She was handsomer than ever, with her two babies at her knee—perfect mother as she was perfect wife. Poor Paul! I wonder if he ever dreamed what a flower was hidden in the folded bud?

Not long after their arrival, I dined alone with the Halidons, and lingered on to smoke with Ned while his wife went alone to the opera. He seemed dull and out of sorts, and complained of a twinge of gout.

"Fact is, I don't get enough exercise—I must look about for a horse."

He had gone afoot for a good many years, and kept his clear skin and quick eye on that homely regimen—but I had to remind myself that, after all, we were both older; and also that the Halidons had champagne every evening.

"How do you like these cigars? They're some I've just got out from London, but I'm not quite satisfied with them myself," he grumbled, pushing toward me the silver box and its attendant taper.

I leaned to the flame, and our eyes met as I lit my cigar. Ned flushed and laughed uneasily. "Poor Paul! Were you thinking of those execrable weeds of his?—I wonder how I knew you were? Probably because I have been wanting to talk to you of our plan—I sent Daisy off alone so that we might have a quiet evening. Not that she isn't interested, only the technical details bore her."

I hesitated. "Are there many technical details left to settle?"

Halidon pushed his armchair back from the fire-light, and twirled his cigar between his fingers. "I didn't suppose there were till I began to look into things a little more closely. You know I never had much of a head for business, and it was chiefly with you that Paul used to go over the figures."

"The figures—?"

"There it is, you see." He paused. "Have you any idea how much this thing is going to cost?"

"Approximately, yes."

"And have you any idea how much we—how much Daisy's fortune amounts to?"

"None whatever," I hastened to assert.

He looked relieved. "Well, we simply can't do it—and live."

"Live?"

"Paul didn't *live*," he said impatiently. "I can't ask a woman with two children to think of—hang it, she's under no actual obligation—" He rose and began to walk the floor. Presently he paused and halted in front of me, defensively, as Paul had once done years before. "It's not that I've lost the sense of *my* obligation—it grows keener with the growth of my happiness; but my position's a delicate one—"

"Ah, my dear fellow—"

"You *do* see it? I knew you would." (Yes, he was duller!) "That's the point. I can't strip my wife and children to carry out a plan—a plan so nebulous that even its inventor. . . . The long and short of it is that the whole scheme must be re-studied, reorganized. Paul lived in a world of dreams."

I rose and tossed my cigar into the fire. "There were some things he never dreamed of," I said.

Halidon rose too, facing me uneasily. "You mean—?"

"That *you* would taunt him with not having spent that money."

He pulled himself up with darkening brows; then the muscles of his forehead relaxed, a flush suffused it, and he held out his hand in boyish penitence.

"I stand a good deal from you," he said.

He kept up his idea of going over the Academy question—threshing it out once for all, as he expressed it; but my suggestion that we should provisionally resuscitate the extinct board did not meet with his approval.

"Not till the whole business is settled. I shouldn't have the face— Wait till I can go to them and say: 'We're laying the foundation-stone on such a day.'"

We had one or two conferences, and Ned speedily lost himself in a maze of figures. His nimble fancy was recalcitrant to mental discipline, and he excused his inattention with the plea that he had no head for business.

"All I know is that it's a colossal undertaking, and that short of living on bread and water—" and then we turned anew to the hard problem of retrenchment.

At the close of the second conference we fixed a date for a third, when Ned's business adviser was to be called in; but before the day came, I learned casually that the Halidons had gone south. Some weeks later Ned wrote me from Florida, apologizing for his remissness. They had rushed off suddenly—his wife had a cough, he explained.

When they returned in the spring, I heard that they had bought the Brereton house, for what seemed to my inexperienced ears a very large sum. But Ned, whom I met one day at the club, explained to me convincingly that it was really the most economical thing they could do. "You don't understand about such things, dear boy, living in your Diogenes tub; but wait till there's a Mrs. Diogenes. I can assure you it's a lot cheaper than building, which is what Daisy would have preferred, and of course," he added, his color rising as our eyes met, "of course, once the Academy's going, I shall have to make my head-quarters here; and I suppose even you won't grudge me a roof over my head."

The Brereton roof was a vast one, with a marble balustrade about it; and I could quite understand, without Ned's halting explanation, that "under the circumstances" it would be necessary to defer what he called "our work—" "Of course, after we've rallied from this amputation, we shall grow fresh supplies—I mean my wife's investments will," he laughingly corrected, "and then we'll have no big outlays ahead and shall know exactly where we stand. After all, my dear fellow, charity begins at home!"

IV

THE Halidons floated off to Europe for the summer. In due course their return was announced in the social chronicle, and walking up Fifth Avenue one afternoon I saw the back of the Brereton house sheathed in scaffolding, and realized that they were adding a wing.

I did not look up Halidon, nor did I hear from him till the middle of the winter. Once or twice, meanwhile, I had seen him in the back of his wife's opera box; but Mrs. Halidon had grown so resplendent that she reduced her handsome husband to a supernumerary. In January the papers began to talk of the Halidon ball; and in due course I received a card for it. I was not a frequenter of balls, and had no intention of going to this one; but when the day came some obscure impulse moved me to set aside my rule, and toward midnight I presented myself at Ned's illuminated portals.

I shall never forget his look when I accosted him on the threshold of the big new ballroom. With celibate egoism I had rather fancied he would be gratified by my departure from custom; but one glance showed me my mistake. He smiled warmly, indeed, and threw into his handclasp an artificial energy of welcome—"You of all people—my dear fellow! Have you seen Daisy?"—but the look behind the smile made me feel cold in the crowded room.

Nor was Mrs. Halidon's greeting calculated to restore my circulation. "Have you come to spy on us?" her frosty smile seemed to say; and I crept home early, wondering if she had not found me out.

It was the following week that Halidon turned up one day in my office. He looked pale and thinner, and for the first time I noticed a dash of gray in his hair. I was startled at the change in him, but I reflected that it was nearly a year since we had looked at each other by daylight, and that my shaving-glass had doubtless a similar tale to tell.

He fidgeted about the office, told me a funny story about his little boy, and then dropped into a chair.

"Look here," he said, "I want to go into business."

"Business?" I stared.

"Well, why not? I suppose men have gone to work, even at my age, and not made a complete failure of it. The fact is, I want to make some money." He paused, and added: "I've heard of an opportunity to pick up for next to nothing a site for the Academy, and if I could lay my hands on a little cash—"

"Do you want to speculate?" I interposed.

"Heaven forbid! But don't you see that, if I had a fixed job—so much a quarter—I could borrow the money and pay it off gradually?"

I meditated upon this astounding proposition. "Do you really think it's wise to buy a site before—"

"Before what?"

"Well—seeing ahead a little?"

His face fell for a moment, but he rejoined cheerfully: "It's an exceptional chance, and after all, I *shall* see ahead if I can get regular work. I can put by a little every month, and by and bye, when our living expenses diminish, my wife means to come forward—her idea would be to give the building—"

He broke off and drummed on the table, waiting nervously for me to speak. He did not say on what grounds he still counted on a diminution of his household expenses, and I had not the cruelty to press this point; but I murmured, after a moment: "I think you're right—I should try to buy the land."

We discussed his potentialities for work, which were obviously still an unknown quantity, and the conference ended in my sending him to a firm of real-estate brokers who were looking out for a partner with a little money to invest. Halidon had a few thousands of his own, which he decided to embark in the venture; and thereafter, for the remaining months of the winter, he appeared punctually at a desk in the brokers' office, and sketched plans of the Academy on the back of their business paper. The site for the future building had meanwhile been bought, and I rather deplored the publicity which Ned gave to the fact; but, after all, since this publicity served to commit him more deeply, to pledge him conspicuously to the completion of his task, it was perhaps a wise instinct of self-coercion that had prompted him.

It was a dull winter in realty, and toward spring, when the market began to revive, one of the Halidon children showed symptoms of a delicate throat, and the fashionable doctor who humoured the family ailments counselled—nay, commanded—a prompt flight to the Mediterranean.

"He says a New York spring would be simply criminal—and as for those ghastly southern places, my wife won't hear of them; so we're off. But I shall be back in July, and I mean to stick to the office all summer."

He was true to his word, and reappeared just as all his friends were deserting town. For two torrid months he sat at his desk, drawing fresh plans of the Academy, and waiting for the wind-fall of a "big deal"; but in September he broke down from the effect of the unwonted confinement, and his indignant wife swept him off to the mountains.

"Why Ned should work when we have the money—I wish he would sell that wretched piece of land!" And sell it he did one day: I chanced on a record of the transaction in the realty column of the morning paper. He afterward explained the sale to me at length. Owing to some spasmodic effort at municipal improvement, there had been an unforeseen rise in the adjoining property, and it would have been foolish—yes, I agreed that it would have been foolish. He had made $10,000 on the sale, and that would go toward paying off what he had borrowed for the original purchase. Meanwhile he could be looking about for another site.

Later in the winter he told me it was a bad time to look. His position in the real-estate business enabled him to follow the trend of the market, and that trend was obstinately upward. But of course there would be a reaction—and he was keeping his eyes open.

As the resuscitated Academy scheme once more fell into abeyance, I saw Halidon less and less frequently; and we had not met for several months, when one day of June, my morning paper startled me with the announcement that the President had appointed Edward Halidon of New York to be Civil Commissioner of our newly acquired Eastern possession, the Manana Islands. "The unhealthy climate of the islands, and the defective sanitation of the towns, make it necessary that vigorous measures should be taken to protect the health of the American citizens established there, and it is believed that Mr. Halidon's large experience of Eastern life and well-known energy of character—" I read the paragraph twice; then I dropped the paper, and projected myself through the subway to Halidon's office. But he was not there; he had not been there for a month. One of the clerks believed he was in Washington.

"It's true, then!" I said to myself. "But Mrs. Halidon in the Mananas—?"

A day or two later Ned appeared in my office. He looked better than when we had last met, and there was a determined line about his lips.

"My wife? Heaven forbid! You don't suppose I should think of taking her? But the job is a tremendously interesting one, and it's the kind of work I believe I can do—the only kind," he added, smiling rather ruefully.

"But my dear Ned—"

He faced me with a look of quiet resolution. "I think I've been through all the *buts*. It's an infernal climate, of course, but then I am used to the East—I know what precautions to take. And it would be a big thing to clean up that Augean stable."

"But consider your wife and children—"

He met this with deliberation. "I *have* considered my children—that's the point. I don't want them to be able to say, when they look back: 'He was content to go on living on that money—'"

"My dear Ned—"

"That's the one thing they *shan't* say of me," he pressed on vehemently. "I've tried other ways—but I'm no good at business. I see now that I shall never make money enough to carry out the scheme myself; but at least I can clear out, and not go on being *his* pensioner—seeing his dreams turned into horses and carpets and clothes—"

He broke off, and leaning on my desk hid his face in his hands. When he looked up again his flush of wrath had subsided.

"Just understand me—it's not *her* fault. Don't fancy I'm trying for an instant to shift the blame. A woman with children simply obeys the instinct of her sex; she puts them first—and I wouldn't have it otherwise. As far as she's concerned there were no conditions attached—there's no reason why she should make any sacrifice." He paused, and added painfully: "The trouble is, I can't make her see that I am differently situated."

"But, Ned, the climate—what are you going to gain by chucking yourself away?"

He lifted his brows. "That's a queer argument from *you*. And, besides, I'm up to the tricks of all those ague-holes. And I've *got* to live, you see: I've got something to put through." He saw my look of enquiry, and added with a shy, poignant laugh—how I hear it still!—: "I don't mean only the job in hand, though that's enough in itself; but Paul's work—you understand.—It won't come in *my* day, of course—I've got to accept that—but my boy's a splendid chap" (the boy was three), "and I tell you what it is, old man, I believe when he grows up *he'll put it through*."

Halidon went to the Mananas, and for two years the journals brought me incidental reports of the work he was accomplishing. He certainly had found a job to his hand: official words of commendation rang through the country, and there were lengthy newspaper leaders on the efficiency with which our representative was prosecuting his task in that lost corner of our colonies. Then one day a brief paragraph announced his death—"one of the last victims of the pestilence he had so successfully combated."

That evening, at my club, I heard men talking of him. One said: "What's the use of a fellow wasting himself on a lot of savages?" and another wiseacre opined: "Oh, he went off because there was friction at home. A fellow like that, who knew the East, would have got through all right if he'd taken the proper precautions. I saw him before he left, and I never saw a man look less as if he wanted to live."

I turned on the last speaker, and my voice made him drop his lighted cigar on his complacent knuckles.

"I never knew a man," I exclaimed, "who had better reasons for wanting to live!"

A handsome youth mused: "Yes, his wife is very beautiful—but it doesn't follow—"

And then some one nudged him, for they knew I was Halidon's friend.

THE PRETEXT

I

Mrs. Ransom, when the front door had closed on her visitor, passed with a spring from the drawing-room to the narrow hall, and thence up the narrow stairs to her bedroom.

Though slender, and still light of foot, she did not always move so quickly: hitherto, in her life, there had not been much to hurry for, save the recurring domestic tasks that compel haste without fostering elasticity; but some impetus of youth revived, communicated to her by her talk with Guy Dawnish, now found expression in her girlish flight upstairs, her girlish impatience to bolt herself into her room with her throbs and her blushes.

Her blushes? Was she really blushing?

She approached the cramped eagle-topped mirror above her plain prim dressing-table: just such a meagre concession to the weakness of the flesh as every old-fashioned house in Wentworth counted among its relics. The face reflected in this unflattering surface—for even the mirrors of Wentworth erred on the side of depreciation—did not seem, at first sight, a suitable theatre for the display of the tenderer emotions, and its owner blushed more deeply as the fact was forced upon her.

Her fair hair had grown too thin—it no longer quite hid the blue veins in her candid forehead—a forehead that one seemed to see turned toward professorial desks, in large bare halls where a snowy winter light fell uncompromisingly on rows of "thoughtful women." Her mouth was thin, too, and a little strained; her lips were too pale; and there were lines in the corners of her eyes. It was a face which had grown middle-aged while it waited for the joys of youth.

Well—but if she could still blush? Instinctively she drew back a little, so that her scrutiny became less microscopic, and the pretty lingering pink threw a veil over her pallor, the hollows in her temples, the faint wrinkles of inexperience about her lips and eyes. How a little colour helped! It made her eyes so deep and shining. She saw now why bad women rouged. . . . Her redness deepened at the thought.

But suddenly she noticed for the first time that the collar of her dress was cut too low. It showed the shrunken lines of the throat. She rummaged feverishly in a tidy scentless drawer, and snatching out a bit of black velvet, bound it about her neck. Yes—that was better. It gave her the relief she needed. Relief—contrast—that was it! She had never had any, either in her appearance or in her setting. She was as flat as the pattern of the wall-paper—and so was her life. And all the people about her had the same look. Wentworth was the kind of place where husbands and wives gradually grew to resemble each other—one or two of her friends, she remembered, had told her lately that she and Ransom were beginning to look alike. . . .

But why had she always, so tamely, allowed her aspect to conform to her situation? Perhaps a gayer exterior would have provoked a brighter fate. Even now—she turned back to the glass, loosened the tight strands of hair above her brow, ran the fine end of the comb under them with a rapid frizzing motion, and then disposed them, more lightly and amply, above her eager face. Yes—it was really better; it made a difference. She smiled at herself with a timid coquetry, and her lips seemed rosier as she smiled. Then she laid down the comb and the smile faded. It made a difference, certainly—but was it right to try to make one's hair look thicker and wavier than it really was? Between that and rouging the ethical line seemed almost impalpable, and the spectre of her rigid New England ancestry rose reprovingly before her. She was sure that none of her grandmothers had ever simulated a curl or encouraged a blush. A blush, indeed! What had any of them ever had to blush for in all their frozen lives? And what, in Heaven's name, had she? She sat down in the stiff mahogany rocking-chair beside her work-table and tried to collect herself. From childhood she had been taught to "collect herself"—but never before had her small sensations and aspirations been so widely scattered, diffused over so vague and uncharted an expanse. Hitherto they had lain in neatly sorted and easily accessible bundles on the high shelves of a perfectly ordered moral consciousness. And now—now that for the first time they *needed* collecting—now that the little winged and scattered bits of self were dancing madly down the vagrant winds of fancy, she knew no spell to call them to the fold again. The best way, no doubt—if only her bewilderment permitted—was to go back to the beginning—the beginning, at least, of to-day's visit—to recapitulate, word for word and look for look. . . .

She clasped her hands on the arms of the chair, checked its swaying with a firm thrust of her foot, and fixed her eyes upon the inward vision. . . .

To begin with, what had made to-day's visit so different from the others? It became suddenly vivid to her that there had been many, almost daily, others, since Guy Dawnish's coming to Wentworth. Even the previous winter—the winter of his arrival from England—his visits had been numerous enough to make Wentworth aware that—very naturally—Mrs. Ransom was "looking after" the stray young Englishman committed to her husband's care by an eminent Q. C. whom the Ransoms had known on one of their brief London visits, and with whom Ransom had since maintained professional relations. All this was in the natural order of things, as sanctioned by the social code of Wentworth. Every one was kind to Guy Dawnish—some rather importunately so, as Margaret Ransom had smiled to observe—but it was recognized as fitting that she should be kindest, since he was in a sense her property, since his people in England, by profusely acknowledging her kindness, had given it the domestic sanction without which, to Wentworth, any social relation between the sexes remained unhallowed and to be viewed askance. Yes! And even this second winter, when the visits had become so much more frequent, so admitted a part of the day's routine, there had not been, from any one, a hint of surprise or of conjecture. . . .

Mrs. Ransom smiled with a faint bitterness. She was protected by her age, no doubt—her age and her past, and the image her mirror gave back to her. . . .

Her door-handle turned suddenly, and the bolt's resistance was met by an impatient knock.

"Margaret!"

She started up, her brightness fading, and unbolted the door to admit her husband.

"Why are you locked in? Why, you're not dressed yet!" he exclaimed.

It was possible for Ransom to reach his dressing-room by a slight circuit through the passage; but it was characteristic of the relentless domesticity of their relation that he chose, as a matter of course, the director way through his wife's bedroom. She had never before been disturbed by this practice, which she accepted as inevitable, but had merely adapted her own habits to it, delaying her hasty toilet till he was safely in his room, or completing it before she heard his step on the stair;

since a scrupulous traditional prudery had miraculously survived this massacre of all the privacies.

"Oh, I shan't dress this evening—I shall just have some tea in the library after you've gone," she answered absently. "Your things are laid out," she added, rousing herself.

He looked surprised. "The dinner's at seven. I suppose the speeches will begin at nine. I thought you were coming to hear them."

She wavered. "I don't know. I think not. Mrs. Sperry's ill, and I've no one else to go with."

He glanced at his watch. "Why not get hold of Dawnish? Wasn't he here just now? Why didn't you ask him?"

She turned toward her dressing-table, and straightened the comb and brush with a nervous hand. Her husband had given her, that morning, two tickets for the ladies' gallery in Hamblin Hall, where the great public dinner of the evening was to take place—a banquet offered by the faculty of Wentworth to visitors of academic eminence—and she had meant to ask Dawnish to go with her: it had seemed the most natural thing to do, till the end of his visit came, and then, after all, she had not spoken. . . .

"It's too late now," she murmured, bending over her pin cushion.

"Too late? Not if you telephone him."

Her husband came toward her, and she turned quickly to face him, lest he should suspect her of trying to avoid his eye. To what duplicity was she already committed!

Ransom laid a friendly hand on her arm: "Come along, Margaret. You know I speak for the bar." She was aware, in his voice, of a little note of surprise at his having to remind her of this.

"Oh, yes. I meant to go, of course—"

"Well, then—" He opened his dressing-room door, and caught a glimpse of the retreating house-maid's skirt. "Here's Maria now. Maria! Call up Mr. Dawnish—at Mrs. Creswell's, you know. Tell him Mrs. Ransom wants him to go with her to hear the speeches this evening—the *speeches*, you understand?—and he's to call for her at a quarter before nine."

Margaret heard the Irish "Yessir" on the stairs, and stood motionless, while her husband added loudly: "And bring me some towels when you come up." Then he turned back into his wife's room.

"Why, it would be a thousand pities for Guy to miss this. He's so interested in the way we do things over here—and I don't know that he's ever heard me speak in public." Again the slight note of fatuity! Was it possible that Ransom was a fatuous man?

He paused in front of her, his short-sighted unobservant glance concentrating itself unexpectedly on her face.

"You're not going like that, are you?" he asked, with glaring eye-glasses.

"Like what?" she faltered, lifting a conscious hand to the velvet at her throat.

"With your hair in such a fearful mess. Have you been shampooing it? You look like the Brant girl at the end of a tennis-match."

The Brant girl was their horror—the horror of all right-thinking Wentworth; a laced, whale-boned, frizzle-headed, high-heeled daughter of iniquity, who came—from New York, of course—on long, disturbing, tumultuous visits to a Wentworth aunt, working havoc among the freshmen, and leaving, when she departed, an angry wake of criticism that ruffled the social waters for weeks. *She*, too, had tried her hand at Guy—with ludicrous unsuccess. And now, to be compared to her—to be accused of looking "New Yorky!" Ah, there are times when husbands are obtuse; and Ransom, as he stood there, thick and yet juiceless, in his dry legal middle age, with his wiry dust-coloured beard, and his perpetual *pince-nez*, seemed to his wife a sudden embodiment of this traditional attribute. Not that she had ever fancied herself, poor soul, a *"femme incomprise."* She had, on the contrary, prided herself on being understood by her husband, almost as much as on her own complete comprehension of him. Wentworth laid a good deal of stress on "motives"; and Margaret Ransom and her husband had dwelt in a complete community of motive. It had been the proudest day of her life when, without consulting her, he had refused an offer of partnership in an eminent New York firm because he preferred the distinction of practising in Wentworth, of being known as the legal representative of the University. Wentworth, in fact, had always been the bond between the two; they were united in their veneration for that estimable seat of learning, and in their modest yet vivid consciousness of possessing its tone. The Wentworth "tone" is unmistakable: it permeates every part of the social economy, from the *coiffure* of the ladies to the preparation of the food. It has its sumptuary laws as well as its curriculum of learning. It sits in judgment not only on its own townsmen but on the rest of the world—enlightening, criticising, ostracizing a heedless universe—and non-conformity to Wentworth standards involves obliteration from Wentworth's consciousness.

In a world without traditions, without reverence, without stability, such little expiring centres of prejudice and precedent make an irresistible appeal to those instincts for which a democracy has neglected to provide. Wentworth, with its "tone," its backward references, its inflexible aversions and condemnations, its hard moral outline preserved intact against a whirling background of experiment, had been all the poetry and history of Margaret Ransom's life. Yes, what she had really esteemed in her husband was the fact of his being so intense an embodiment of Wentworth; so long and closely identified, for instance, with its legal affairs, that he was almost a part of its university existence, that of course, at a college banquet, he would inevitably speak for the bar!

It was wonderful of how much consequence all this had seemed till now. . . .

II

WHEN, punctually at ten minutes to seven, her husband had emerged from the house, Margaret Ransom remained seated in her bedroom, addressing herself anew to the difficult process of self-collection. As an aid to this endeavour, she bent forward and looked out of the window, following Ransom's figure as it receded down the elm-shaded street. He moved almost alone between the prim flowerless grass-plots, the white porches, the protrusion of irrelevant shingled gables, which stamped the empty street as part of an American college town. She had always been proud of living in Hill Street, where the university people congregated, proud to associate her husband's retreating back, as he walked daily to his office, with backs literary and pedagogic, backs of which it was whispered, for the edification of duly-impressed visitors: "Wait till that old boy turns—that's so-and-so."

This had been her world, a world destitute of personal experience, but filled with a rich sense of privilege and distinction, of being not as those millions were who, denied the inestimable advantage of living at Wentworth, pursued elsewhere careers foredoomed to futility by that very fact.

And now—!

She rose and turned to her work-table where she had dropped, on entering, the handful of photographs that Guy Dawnish had left with her. While he sat so close, pointing out and explaining, she had hardly taken in the details; but now, on the full tones of his low young voice, they came back with redoubled distinctness. This was Guise Abbey, his uncle's place in Wiltshire, where, under his grandfather's rule, Guy's own boyhood had been spent: a long gabled Jacobean facade, many-chimneyed, ivy-draped, overhung (she felt sure) by the boughs of a venerable rookery. And in this other picture—the walled garden at Guise—that was his uncle, Lord Askern, a hale gouty-looking figure, planted robustly on the terrace, a gun on his shoulder and a couple of setters at his feet. And here was the river below the park, with Guy "punting" a girl in a flapping hat—how Margaret hated the flap that hid the girl's face! And here was the tennis-court, with Guy among a jolly cross-legged group of youths in flannels, and pretty girls about the tea-table under the big lime: in the centre the curate handing bread and butter, and in the middle distance a footman approaching with more cups.

Margaret raised this picture closer to her eyes, puzzling, in the diminished light, over the face of the girl nearest to Guy Dawnish—bent above him in profile, while he laughingly lifted his head. No hat hid this profile, which stood out clearly against the foliage behind it.

"And who is that handsome girl?" Margaret had said, detaining the photograph as he pushed it aside, and struck by the fact that, of the whole group, he had left only this member unnamed.

"Oh, only Gwendolen Matcher—I've always known her—. Look at this: the almshouses at Guise. Aren't they jolly?"

And then—without her having had the courage to ask if the girl in the punt were also Gwendolen Matcher—they passed on to photographs of his rooms at Oxford, of a cousin's studio in London—one of Lord Askern's grandsons was "artistic"—of the rose-hung cottage in Wales to which, on the old Earl's death, his daughter-in-law, Guy's mother, had retired.

Every one of the photographs opened a window on the life Margaret had been trying to picture since she had known him—a life so rich, so romantic, so packed—in the mere casual vocabulary of daily life—with historic reference and poetic allusion, that she felt almost oppressed by this distant whiff of its air. The very words he used fascinated and bewildered her. He seemed to have been born into all sorts of connections, political, historical, official, that made the Ransom situation at Wentworth as featureless as the top shelf of a dark closet. Some one in the family had "asked for the Chiltern Hundreds"—one uncle was an Elder Brother of the Trinity House—some one else was the Master of a College—some one was in command at Devonport—the Army, the Navy, the House of Commons, the House of Lords, the most venerable seats of learning, were all woven into the dense background of this young man's light unconscious talk. For the unconsciousness was unmistakable. Margaret was not without experience of the transatlantic visitor who sounds loud names and evokes reverberating connections. The poetry of Guy Dawnish's situation lay in the fact that it was so completely a part of early associations and accepted facts. Life was like that in England—in Wentworth of course (where he had been sent, through his uncle's influence, for two years' training in the neighbouring electrical works at Smedden)—in Wentworth, though "immensely jolly," it was different. The fact that he was qualifying to be an electrical engineer—with the hope of a secretaryship at the London end of the great Smedden Company—that, at best, he was returning home to a life of industrial "grind," this fact, though avowedly a bore, did not disconnect him from that brilliant pinnacled past, that many-faceted life in which the brightest episodes of the whole body of English fiction seemed collectively reflected. Of course he would have to work—younger sons' sons almost always had to—but his uncle Askern (like Wentworth) was "immensely jolly," and Guise always open to him, and his other uncle, the Master, a capital old boy too—and in town he could always put up with his clever aunt, Lady Caroline Duckett, who had made a "beastly marriage" and was horribly poor, but who knew everybody jolly and amusing, and had always been particularly kind to him.

It was not—and Margaret had not, even in her own thoughts, to defend herself from the imputation—it was not what Wentworth would have called the "material side" of her friend's situation that captivated her. She was austerely proof against such appeals: her enthusiasms were all of the imaginative order. What subjugated her was the unexampled prodigality with which he poured for her the same draught of tradition of which Wentworth held out its little teacupful. He besieged her with a million Wentworths in one—saying, as it were: "All these are mine for the asking—and I choose you instead!"

For this, she told herself somewhat dizzily, was what it came to—the summing-up toward which her conscientious efforts at self-collection had been gradually pushing her: with all this in reach, Guy Dawnish was leaving Wentworth reluctantly.

"I *was* a bit lonely here at first—but *now!*" And again: "It will be jolly, of course, to see them all again—but there are some things one doesn't easily give up...."

If he had known only Wentworth, it would have been wonderful enough that he should have chosen her out of all Wentworth—but to have known that other life, and to set her in the balance against it—poor Margaret Ransom, in whom, at the moment, nothing seemed of weight but her years! Ah, it might well produce, in nerves and brain, and poor unpractised pulses, a flushed tumult of sensation, the rush of a great wave of life, under which memory struggled in vain to reassert itself, to particularize again just what his last words—the very last—had been. . . .

When consciousness emerged, quivering, from this retrospective assault, it pushed Margaret Ransom—feeling herself a mere leaf in the blast—toward the writing-table from which her innocent and voluminous correspondence habitually flowed. She had a letter to write now—much shorter but more difficult than any she had ever been called on to indite.

"Dear Mr. Dawnish," she began, "since telephoning you just now I have decided not—"

Maria's voice, at the door, announced that tea was in the library: "And I s'pose it's the brown silk you'll wear to the speaking?"

In the usual order of the Ransom existence, its mistress's toilet was performed unassisted; and the mere enquiry—at once friendly and deferential—projected, for Margaret, a strong light on the importance of the occasion. That she should answer: "But I am not going," when the going was so manifestly part of a household solemnity about which the thoughts below stairs fluttered in proud participation; that in face of such participation she should utter a word implying indifference or hesitation—nay, revealing herself the transposed, uprooted thing she had been on the verge of becoming; to do this was—well! infinitely harder than to perform the alternative act of tearing up the sheet of note-paper under her reluctant pen.

Yes, she said, she would wear the brown silk. . . .

III

ALL the heat and glare from the long illuminated table, about which the fumes of many courses still hung in a savoury fog, seemed to surge up to the ladies' gallery, and concentrate themselves in the burning cheeks of a slender figure withdrawn behind the projection of a pillar.

It never occurred to Margaret Ransom that she was sitting in the shade. She supposed that the full light of the chandeliers was beating on her face—and there were moments when it seemed as though all the heads about the great horse-shoe below, bald, shaggy, sleek, close-thatched, or thinly latticed, were equipped with an additional pair of eyes, set at an angle which enabled them to rake her face as relentlessly as the electric burners.

In the lull after a speech, the gallery was fluttering with the rustle of programmes consulted, and Mrs. Sheff (the Brant girl's aunt) leaned forward to say enthusiastically: "And now we're to hear Mr. Ransom!"

A louder buzz rose from the table, and the heads (without relaxing their upward vigilance) seemed to merge, and flow together, like an attentive flood, toward the upper end of the horse-shoe, where all the threads of Margaret Ransom's consciousness were suddenly drawn into what seemed a small speck, no more—a black speck that rose, hung in air, dissolved into gyrating gestures, became distended, enormous, preponderant—became her husband "speaking."

"It's the heat—" Margaret gasped, pressing her handkerchief to her whitening lips, and finding just strength enough left to push back farther into the shadow.

She felt a touch on her arm. "It *is* horrible—shall we go?" a voice suggested; and, "Yes, yes, let us go," she whispered, feeling, with a great throb of relief, *that* to be the only possible, the only conceivable, solution. To sit and listen to her husband *now*—how could she ever have thought she could survive it? Luckily, under the lingering hubbub from below, his opening words were inaudible, and she had only to run the gauntlet of sympathetic feminine glances, shot after her between waving fans and programmes, as, guided by Guy Dawnish, she managed to reach the door. It was really so hot that even Mrs. Sheff was not much surprised—till long afterward. . . .

The winding staircase was empty, half dark and blessedly silent. In a committee room below Dawnish found the inevitable water jug, and filled a glass for her, while she leaned back, confronted only by a frowning college President in an emblazoned frame. The academic frown descended on her like an anathema when she rose and followed her companion out of the building.

Hamblin Hall stands at the end of the long green "Campus" with its sextuple line of elms—the boast and the singularity of Wentworth. A pale spring moon, rising above the dome of the University library at the opposite end of the elm-walk, diffused a pearly mildness in the sky, melted to thin haze the shadows of the trees, and turned to golden yellow the lights of the college windows. Against this soft suffusion of light the Library cupola assumed a Bramantesque grace, the white steeple of the congregational church became a campanile topped by a winged spirit, and the scant porticoes of the older halls the colonnades of classic temples.

"This is better—" Dawnish said, as they passed down the steps and under the shadow of the elms.

They moved on a little way in silence before he began again: "You're too tired to walk. Let us sit down a few minutes."

Her feet, in truth, were leaden, and not far off a group of park benches, encircling the pedestal of a patriot in bronze, invited them to rest. But Dawnish was guiding her toward a lateral path which bent, through shrubberies, toward a strip of turf between two of the buildings.

"It will be cooler by the river," he said, moving on without waiting for a possible protest. None came: it seemed easier, for the moment, to let herself be led without any conventional feint of resistance. And besides, there was nothing wrong about *this*—the wrong would have been in sitting up there in the glare, pretending to listen to her husband, a dutiful wife among her kind. . . .

The path descended, as both knew, to the chosen, the inimitable spot of Wentworth: that fugitive curve of the river, where, before hurrying on to glut the brutal industries of South Wentworth and Smedden, it simulated for a few hundred yards the leisurely pace of an ancient university stream, with willows on its banks and a stretch of turf extending from the grounds of Hamblin Hall to the boat houses at the farther bend. Here too were benches, beneath the willows, and so close to the river that the voice of its gliding softened and filled out the reverberating silence between Margaret and her companion, and made her feel that she knew why he had brought her there.

"Do you feel better?" he asked gently as he sat down beside her.

"Oh, yes. I only needed a little air."

"I'm so glad you did. Of course the speeches were tremendously interesting—but I prefer this. What a good night!"

"Yes."

There was a pause, which now, after all, the soothing accompaniment of the river seemed hardly sufficient to fill.

"I wonder what time it is. I ought to be going home," Margaret began at length.

"Oh, it's not late. They'll be at it for hours in there—yet."

She made a faint inarticulate sound. She wanted to say: "No—Robert's speech was to be the last—" but she could not bring herself to pronounce Ransom's name, and at the moment no other way of refuting her companion's statement occurred to her.

The young man leaned back luxuriously, reassured by her silence.

"You see it's my last chance—and I want to make the most of it."

"Your last chance?" How stupid of her to repeat his words on that cooing note of interrogation! It was just such a lead as the Brant girl might have given him.

"To be with you—like this. I haven't had so many. And there's less than a week left."

She attempted to laugh. "Perhaps it will sound longer if you call it five days."

The flatness of that, again! And she knew there were people who called her intelligent. Fortunately he did not seem to notice it; but her laugh continued to sound in her own ears—the coquettish chirp of middle age! She decided that if he spoke again—if he *said anything*—she would make no farther effort at evasion: she would take it directly, seriously, frankly—she would not be doubly disloyal.

"Besides," he continued, throwing his arm along the back of the bench, and turning toward her so that his face was like a dusky bas-relief with a silver rim—"besides, there's something I've been wanting to tell you."

The sound of the river seemed to cease altogether: the whole world became silent.

Margaret had trusted her inspiration farther than it appeared likely to carry her. Again she could think of nothing happier than to repeat, on the same witless note of interrogation: "To tell me?"

"You only."

The constraint, the difficulty, seemed to be on his side now: she divined it by the renewed shifting of his attitude—he was capable, usually, of such fine intervals of immobility—and by a confusion in his utterance that set her own voice throbbing in her throat.

"You've been so perfect to me," he began again. "It's not my fault if you've made me feel that you would understand everything—make allowances for everything—see just how a man may have held out, and fought against a thing—as long as he had the strength. . . . This may be my only chance; and I can't go away without telling you."

He had turned from her now, and was staring at the river, so that his profile was projected against the moonlight in all its beautiful young dejection.

There was a slight pause, as though he waited for her to speak; then she leaned forward and laid her hand on his.

"If I have really been—if I have done for you even the least part of what you say . . . what you imagine . . . will you do for me, now, just one thing in return?"

He sat motionless, as if fearing to frighten away the shy touch on his hand, and she left it there, conscious of her gesture only as part of the high ritual of their farewell.

"What do you want me to do?" he asked in a low tone.

"*Not* to tell me!" she breathed on a deep note of entreaty.

"*Not* to tell you—?"

"Anything—*anything*—just to leave our . . . our friendship . . . as it has been—as—as a painter, if a friend asked him, might leave a picture—not quite finished, perhaps . . . but all the more exquisite. . . ."

She felt the hand under hers slip away, recover itself, and seek her own, which had flashed out of reach in the same instant—felt the start that swept him round on her as if he had been caught and turned about by the shoulders.

"You—*you*—?" he stammered, in a strange voice full of fear and tenderness; but she held fast, so centred in her inexorable resolve that she was hardly conscious of the effect her words might be producing.

"Don't you see," she hurried on, "don't you *feel* how much safer it is—yes, I'm willing to put it so!—how much safer to leave everything undisturbed . . . just as . . . as it has grown of itself . . . without trying to say: 'It's this or that' . . . ? It's what we each choose to call it to ourselves, after all, isn't it? Don't let us try to find a name that . . . that we should both agree upon . . . we probably shouldn't succeed." She laughed abruptly. "And ghosts vanish when one names them!" she ended with a break in her voice.

When she ceased her heart was beating so violently that there was a rush in her ears like the noise of the river after rain, and she did not immediately make out what he was answering. But as she recovered her lucidity she said to herself that, whatever he was saying, she must not hear it; and she began to speak again, half playfully, half appealingly, with an eloquence of entreaty, an ingenuity in argument, of which she had never dreamed herself capable. And then, suddenly, strangling hands seemed to reach up from her heart to her throat, and she had to stop.

Her companion remained motionless. He had not tried to regain her hand, and his eyes were away from her, on the river. But his nearness had become something formidable and exquisite—something she had never before imagined. A flush of guilt swept over her—vague reminiscences of French novels and of opera plots. This was what such women felt, then . . . this was "shame." . . . Phrases of the newspaper and the pulpit danced before her. . . . She dared not speak, and his silence began to frighten her. Had ever a heart beat so wildly before in Wentworth?

He turned at last, and taking her two hands, quite simply, kissed them one after the other.

"I shall never forget—" he said in a confused voice, unlike his own.

A return of strength enabled her to rise, and even to let her eyes meet his for a moment.

"Thank you," she said, simply also.

She turned away from the bench, regaining the path that led back to the college buildings, and he walked beside her in silence. When they reached the elm walk it was dotted with dispersing groups. The "speaking" was over, and Hamblin Hall had poured its audience out into the moonlight. Margaret felt a rush of relief, followed by a receding wave of regret. She had the distinct sensation that her hour—her one hour—was over.

One of the groups just ahead broke up as they approached, and projected Ransom's solid bulk against the moonlight.

"My husband," she said, hastening forward; and she never afterward forgot the look of his back—heavy, round-shouldered, yet a little pompous—in a badly fitting overcoat that stood out at the neck and hid his collar. She had never before noticed how he dressed.

IV

THEY met again, inevitably, before Dawnish left; but the thing she feared did not happen—he did not try to see her alone.

It even became clear to her, in looking back, that he had deliberately avoided doing so; and this seemed merely an added proof of his "understanding," of that deep undefinable communion that set them alone in an empty world, as if on a peak above the clouds.

The five days passed in a flash; and when the last one came, it brought to Margaret Ransom an hour of weakness, of profound disorganization, when old barriers fell, old convictions faded—when to be alone with him for a moment became, after all, the one craving of her heart. She knew he was coming that afternoon to say "good-by"—and she knew also that Ransom was to be away at South Wentworth. She waited alone in her pale little drawing-room, with its scant kakemonos, its one or two chilly reproductions from the antique, its slippery Chippendale chairs. At length the bell rang, and her world became a rosy blur—through which she presently discerned the austere form of Mrs. Sperry, wife of the Professor of palaeontology, who had come to talk over with her the next winter's programme for the Higher Thought Club. They debated the question for an hour, and when Mrs. Sperry departed Margaret had a confused impression that the course was to deal with the influence of the First Crusade on the development of European architecture—but the sentient part of her knew only that Dawnish had not come.

He "bobbed in," as he would have put it, after dinner—having, it appeared, run across Ransom early in the day, and learned that the latter would be absent till evening. Margaret was in the study with her husband when the door opened and Dawnish stood there. Ransom—who had not had time to dress—was seated at his desk, a pile of shabby law books at his elbow, the light from a hanging lamp falling on his grayish stubble of hair, his sallow forehead and spectacled eyes. Dawnish, towering higher than usual against the shadows of the room, and refined by his unusual pallor, hung a moment on the threshold, then came in, explaining himself profusely—laughing, accepting a cigar, letting Ransom push an arm-chair forward—a Dawnish she had never seen, ill at ease, ejaculatory, yet somehow more mature, more obscurely in command of himself.

Margaret drew back, seating herself in the shade, in such a way that she saw her husband's head first, and beyond it their visitor's, relieved against the dusk of the book shelves. Her heart was still—she felt no throbbing in her throat or temples: all her life seemed concentrated in the hand that lay on her knee, the hand he would touch when they said good-by.

Afterward her heart rang all the changes, and there was a mood in which she reproached herself for cowardice—for having deliberately missed her one moment with him, the moment in which she might have sounded the depths of life, for joy or anguish. But that mood was fleeting and infrequent. In quieter hours she blushed for it—she even trembled to think that he might have guessed such a regret in her. It seemed to convict her of a lack of fineness that he should have had, in his youth and his power, a tenderer, surer sense of the peril of a rash touch—should have handled the case so much more delicately.

At first her days were fire and the nights long solemn vigils. Her thoughts were no longer vulgarized and defaced by any notion of "guilt," of mental disloyalty. She was ashamed now of her shame. What had happened was as much outside the sphere of her marriage as some transaction in a star. It had simply given her a secret life of incommunicable joys, as if all the wasted springs of her youth had been stored in some hidden pool, and she could return there now to bathe in them.

After that there came a phase of loneliness, through which the life about her loomed phantasmal and remote. She thought the dead must feel thus, repeating the vain gestures of the living beside some Stygian shore. She wondered if any other woman had lived to whom *nothing had ever happened?* And then his first letter came. . . .

It was a charming letter—a perfect letter. The little touch of awkwardness and constraint under its boyish spontaneity told her more than whole pages of eloquence. He spoke of their friendship—of their good days together. . . . Ransom, chancing to come in while she read, noticed the foreign stamps; and she was able to hand him the letter, saying gaily: "There's a message for you," and knowing all the while that *her* message was safe in her heart.

On the days when the letters came the outlines of things grew indistinct, and she could never afterward remember what she had done or how the business of life had been carried on. It was always a surprise when she found dinner on the table as usual, and Ransom seated opposite to her, running over the evening paper.

But though Dawnish continued to write, with all the English loyalty to the outward observances of friendship, his communications came only at intervals of several weeks, and between them she had time to repossess herself, to regain some sort of normal contact with life. And the customary, the recurring, gradually reclaimed her, the net of habit tightened again—her daily life became real, and her one momentary escape from it an exquisite illusion. Not that she ceased to believe in the miracle that had befallen her: she still treasured the reality of her one moment beside the river. What reason was there for doubting it? She could hear the ring of truth in young Dawnish's voice: "It's not my fault if you've made me feel that you would understand everything. . . ." No! she believed in her miracle, and the belief sweetened and illumined her life; but she came to see that what was for her the transformation of her whole being might well have been, for her companion, a mere passing explosion of gratitude, of boyish good-fellowship touched with the pang of leave-taking. She even reached the point of telling herself that it was "better so": this view of the episode so defended it from the alternating extremes of self-reproach and derision, so enshrined it in a pale immortality to which she could make her secret pilgrimages without reproach.

For a long time she had not been able to pass by the bench under the willows—she even avoided the elm walk till autumn had stripped its branches. But every day, now, she noted a step toward recovery; and at last a day came when, walking along the river, she said to herself, as she approached the bench: "I used not to be able to pass here without thinking of him; *and now I am not thinking of him at all!*"

This seemed such convincing proof of her recovery that she began, as spring returned, to permit herself, now and then, a quiet session on the bench—a dedicated hour from which she went back fortified to her task.

She had not heard from her friend for six weeks or more—the intervals between his letters were growing longer. But that was "best" too, and she was not anxious, for she knew he had obtained the post he had been preparing for, and that his active life in London had begun. The thought reminded her, one mild March day, that in leaving the house she had thrust in her reticule a letter from a Wentworth friend who was abroad on a holiday. The envelope bore the London post mark, a fact showing that the lady's face was turned toward home. Margaret seated herself on her bench, and drawing out the letter began to read it.

The London described was that of shops and museums—as remote as possible from the setting of Guy Dawnish's existence. But suddenly Margaret's eye fell on his name, and the page began to tremble in her hands.

"I heard such a funny thing yesterday about your friend Mr. Dawnish. We went to a tea at Professor Bunce's (I do wish you knew the Bunces—their atmosphere is so *uplifting*), and there I met that Miss Bruce-Pringle who came out last year to take a course in histology at the Annex. Of course she asked about you and Mr. Ransom, and then she told me she had just seen Mr. Dawnish's aunt—the clever one he was always talking about, Lady Caroline something—and that they were all in a dreadful state about him. I wonder if you knew he was engaged when he went to America? He never mentioned it to *us*. She said it was not a positive engagement, but an understanding with a girl he has always been devoted to, who lives near their place in Wiltshire; and both families expected the marriage to take place as soon as he got back. It seems the girl is an heiress (you know *how low* the English ideals are compared with ours), and Miss Bruce-Pringle said his relations were perfectly delighted at his 'being provided for,' as she called it.

Well, when he got back he asked the girl to release him; and she and her family were furious, and so were his people; but he holds out, and won't marry her, and won't give a reason, except that he has 'formed an unfortunate attachment.' Did you ever hear anything so peculiar? His aunt, who is quite wild about it, says it must have happened at Wentworth, because he didn't go anywhere else in America. Do you suppose it *could* have been the Brant girl? But why 'unfortunate' when everybody knows she would have jumped at him?"

Margaret folded the letter and looked out across the river. It was not the same river, but a mystic current shot with moonlight. The bare willows wove a leafy veil above her head, and beside her she felt the nearness of youth and tempestuous tenderness. It had all happened just here, on this very seat by the river—it had come to her, and passed her by, and she had not held out a hand to detain it. . . .

Well! Was it not, by that very abstention, made more deeply and ineffaceably hers? She could argue thus while she had thought the episode, on his side, a mere transient effect of propinquity; but now that she knew it had altered the whole course of his life, now that it took on substance and reality, asserted a separate existence outside of her own troubled consciousness—now it seemed almost cowardly to have missed her share in it.

She walked home in a dream. Now and then, when she passed an acquaintance, she wondered if the pain and glory were written on her face. But Mrs. Sperry, who stopped her at the corner of Maverick Street to say a word about the next meeting of the Higher Thought Club, seemed to remark no change in her.

When she reached home Ransom had not yet returned from the office, and she went straight to the library to tidy his writing-table. It was part of her daily duty to bring order out of the chaos of his papers, and of late she had fastened on such small recurring tasks as some one falling over a precipice might snatch at the weak bushes in its clefts.

When she had sorted the letters she took up some pamphlets and newspapers, glancing over them to see if they were to be kept. Among the papers was a page torn from a London *Times* of the previous month. Her eye ran down its columns and suddenly a paragraph flamed out.

"We are requested to state that the marriage arranged between Mr. Guy Dawnish, son of the late Colonel the Hon. Roderick Dawnish, of Malby, Wilts, and Gwendolen, daughter of Samuel Matcher, Esq. of Armingham Towers, Wilts, will not take place."

Margaret dropped the paper and sat down, hiding her face against the stained baize of the desk. She remembered the photograph of the tennis-court at Guise—she remembered the handsome girl at whom Guy Dawnish looked up, laughing. A gust of tears shook her, loosening the dry surface of conventional feeling, welling up from unsuspected depths. She was sorry—very sorry, yet so glad—so ineffably, impenitently glad.

V

THERE came a reaction in which she decided to write to him. She even sketched out a letter of sisterly, almost motherly, remonstrance, in which she reminded him that he "still had all his life before him." But she reflected that so, after all, had she; and that seemed to weaken the argument.

In the end she decided not to send the letter. He had never spoken to her of his engagement to Gwendolen Matcher, and his letters had contained no allusion to any sentimental disturbance in his life. She had only his few broken words, that night by the river, on which to build her theory of the case. But illuminated by the phrase "an unfortunate attachment" the theory towered up, distinct and immovable, like some high landmark by which travellers shape their course. She had been loved—extraordinarily loved. But he had chosen that she should know of it by his silence rather than by his speech. He had understood that only on those terms could their transcendant communion continue—that he must lose her to keep her. To break that silence would be like spilling a cup of water in a waste of sand. There would be nothing left for her thirst.

Her life, thenceforward, was bathed in a tranquil beauty. The days flowed by like a river beneath the moon—each ripple caught the brightness and passed it on. She began to take a renewed interest in her familiar round of duties. The tasks which had once seemed colourless and irksome had now a kind of sacrificial sweetness, a symbolic meaning into which she alone was initiated. She had been restless—had longed to travel; now she felt that she should never again care to leave Wentworth. But if her desire to wander had ceased, she travelled in spirit, performing invisible pilgrimages in the footsteps of her friend. She regretted that her one short visit to England had taken her so little out of London—that her acquaintance with the landscape had been formed chiefly through the windows of a railway carriage. She threw herself into the architectural studies of the Higher Thought Club, and distinguished herself, at the spring meetings, by her fluency, her competence, her inexhaustible curiosity on the subject of the growth of English Gothic. She ransacked the shelves of the college library, she borrowed photographs of the cathedrals, she pored over the folio pages of "The Seats of Noblemen and Gentlemen." She was like some banished princess who learns that she has inherited a domain in her own country, who knows that she will never see it, yet feels, wherever she walks, its soil beneath her feet.

May was half over, and the Higher Thought Club was to hold its last meeting, previous to the college festivities which, in early June, agreeably disorganized the social routine of Wentworth. The meeting was to take place in Margaret Ransom's drawing-room, and on the day before she sat upstairs preparing for her dual duties as hostess and orator—for she had been invited to read the final paper of the course. In order to sum up with precision her conclusions on the subject of English Gothic she had been rereading an analysis of the structural features of the principal English cathedrals; and she was murmuring over to herself the phrase: "The longitudinal arches of Lincoln have an approximately elliptical form," when there came a knock on the door, and Maria's voice announced: "There's a lady down in the parlour."

Margaret's soul dropped from the heights of the shadowy vaulting to the dead level of an afternoon call at Wentworth.

"A lady? Did she give no name?"

Maria became confused. "She only said she was a lady—" and in reply to her mistress's look of mild surprise: "Well, ma'am, she told me so three or four times over."

Margaret laid her book down, leaving it open at the description of Lincoln, and slowly descended the stairs. As she did so, she repeated to herself: "The longitudinal arches are elliptical."

On the threshold below, she had the odd impression that her bare and inanimate drawing-room was brimming with life and noise—an impression produced, as she presently perceived, by the resolute forward dash—it was almost a pounce—of the one small figure restlessly measuring its length.

The dash checked itself within a yard of Margaret, and the lady—a stranger—held back long enough to stamp on her hostess a sharp impression of sallowness, leanness, keenness, before she said, in a voice that might have been addressing an unruly committee meeting: "I am

Lady Caroline Duckett—a fact I found it impossible to make clear to the young woman who let me in."

A warm wave rushed up from Margaret's heart to her throat and forehead. She held out both hands impulsively. "Oh, I'm so glad—I'd no idea—"

Her voice sank under her visitor's impartial scrutiny.

"I don't wonder," said the latter drily. "I suppose she didn't mention, either, that my object in calling here was to see Mrs. Ransom?"

"Oh, yes—won't you sit down?" Margaret pushed a chair forward. She seated herself at a little distance, brain and heart humming with a confused interchange of signals. This dark sharp woman was his aunt—the "clever aunt" who had had such a hard life, but had always managed to keep her head above water. Margaret remembered that Guy had spoken of her kindness—perhaps she would seem kinder when they had talked together a little. Meanwhile the first impression she produced was of an amplitude out of all proportion to her somewhat scant exterior. With her small flat figure, her shabby heterogeneous dress, she was as dowdy as any Professor's wife at Wentworth; but her dowdiness (Margaret borrowed a literary analogy to define it), her dowdiness was somehow "of the centre." Like the insignificant emissary of a great power, she was to be judged rather by her passports than her person.

While Margaret was receiving these impressions, Lady Caroline, with quick bird-like twists of her head, was gathering others from the pale void spaces of the drawing-room. Her eyes, divided by a sharp nose like a bill, seemed to be set far enough apart to see at separate angles; but suddenly she bent both of them on Margaret.

"This *is* Mrs. Ransom's house?" she asked, with an emphasis on the verb that gave a distinct hint of unfulfilled expectations.

Margaret assented.

"Because your American houses, especially in the provincial towns, all look so remarkably alike, that I thought I might have been mistaken; and as my time is extremely limited—in fact I'm sailing on Wednesday—"

She paused long enough to let Margaret say: "I had no idea you were in this country."

Lady Caroline made no attempt to take this up. "And so much of it," she carried on her sentence, "has been wasted in talking to people I really hadn't the slightest desire to see, that you must excuse me if I go straight to the point."

Margaret felt a sudden tension of the heart. "Of course," she said while a voice within her cried: "He is dead—he has left me a message."

There was another pause; then Lady Caroline went on, with increasing asperity: "So that—in short—if I *could* see Mrs. Ransom at once—"

Margaret looked up in surprise. "I am Mrs. Ransom," she said.

The other stared a moment, with much the same look of cautious incredulity that had marked her inspection of the drawing-room. Then light came to her.

"Oh, I beg your pardon. I should have said that I wished to see Mrs. *Robert* Ransom, not Mrs. Ransom. But I understood that in the States you don't make those distinctions." She paused a moment, and then went on, before Margaret could answer: "Perhaps, after all, it's as well that I should see you instead, since you're evidently one of the household—your son and his wife live with you, I suppose? Yes, on the whole, then, it's better—I shall be able to talk so much more frankly." She spoke as if, as a rule, circumstances prevented her giving rein to this propensity. "And frankness, of course, is the only way out of this—this extremely tiresome complication. You know, I suppose, that my nephew thinks he's in love with your daughter-in-law?"

Margaret made a slight movement, but her visitor pressed on without heeding it. "Oh, don't fancy, please, that I'm pretending to take a high moral ground—though his mother does, poor dear! I can perfectly imagine that in a place like this—I've just been driving about it for two hours—a young man of Guy's age would *have* to provide himself with some sort of distraction, and he's not the kind to go in for anything objectionable. Oh, we quite allow for that—we should allow for the whole affair, if it hadn't so preposterously ended in his throwing over the girl he was engaged to, and upsetting an arrangement that affected a number of people besides himself. I understand that in the States it's different—the young people have only themselves to consider. In England—in our class, I mean—a great deal may depend on a young man's making a good match; and in Guy's case I may say that his mother and sisters (I won't include myself, though I might) have been simply stranded—thrown overboard—by his freak. You can understand how serious it is when I tell you that it's that and nothing else that has brought me all the way to America. And my first idea was to go straight to your daughter-in-law, since her influence is the only thing we can count on now, and put it to her fairly, as I'm putting it to you. But, on the whole, I dare say it's better to see you first—you might give me an idea of the line to take with her. I'm prepared to throw myself on her mercy!"

Margaret rose from her chair, outwardly rigid in proportion to her inward tremor.

"You don't understand—" she began.

Lady Caroline brushed the interruption aside. "Oh, but I do—completely! I cast no reflection on your daughter-in-law. Guy has made it quite clear to us that his attachment is—has, in short, not been rewarded. But don't you see that that's the worst part of it? There'd be much more hope of his recovering if Mrs. Robert Ransom had—had—"

Margaret's voice broke from her in a cry. "I am Mrs. Robert Ransom," she said.

If Lady Caroline Duckett had hitherto given her hostess the impression of a person not easily silenced, this fact added sensibly to the effect produced by the intense stillness which now fell on her.

She sat quite motionless, her large bangled hands clasped about the meagre fur boa she had unwound from her neck on entering, her rusty black veil pushed up to the edge of a "fringe" of doubtful authenticity, her thin lips parted on a gasp that seemed to sharpen itself on the edges of her teeth. So overwhelming and helpless was her silence that Margaret began to feel a motion of pity beneath her indignation—a desire at least to facilitate the excuses which must terminate their disastrous colloquy. But when Lady Caroline found voice she did not use it to excuse herself.

"You *can't* be," she said, quite simply.

"Can't be?" Margaret stammered, with a flushing cheek.

"I mean, it's some mistake. Are there *two* Mrs. Robert Ransoms in the same town? Your family arrangements are so extremely puzzling." She had a farther rush of enlightenment. "Oh, I *see!* I ought of course to have asked for Mrs. Robert Ransom 'Junior'!"

The idea sent her to her feet with a haste which showed her impatience to make up for lost time.

"There is no other Mrs. Robert Ransom at Wentworth," said Margaret.

"No other—no 'Junior'? Are you *sure?*" Lady Caroline fell back into her seat again. "Then I simply don't see," she murmured helplessly.

Margaret's blush had fixed itself on her throbbing forehead. She remained standing, while her strange visitor continued to gaze at her with a perturbation in which the consciousness of indiscretion had evidently as yet no part.

"I simply don't see," she repeated.

Suddenly she sprang up, and advancing to Margaret laid an inspired hand on her arm. "But, my dear woman, you can help us out all the same; you can help us to find out *who it is*—and you will, won't you? Because, as it's not you, you can't in the least mind what I've been saying—"

Margaret, freeing her arm from her visitor's hold, drew back a step; but Lady Caroline instantly rejoined her.

"Of course, I can see that if it *had* been, you might have been annoyed: I dare say I put the case stupidly—but I'm so bewildered by this new development—by his using you all this time as a pretext—that I really don't know where to turn for light on the mystery—"

She had Margaret in her imperious grasp again, but the latter broke from her with a more resolute gesture.

"I'm afraid I have no light to give you," she began; but once more Lady Caroline caught her up.

"Oh, but do please understand me! I condemn Guy most strongly for using your name—when we all know you'd been so amazingly kind to him! I haven't a word to say in his defence—but of course the important thing now is: *who is the woman, since you're not?*"

The question rang out loudly, as if all the pale puritan corners of the room flung it back with a shudder at the speaker. In the silence that ensued Margaret felt the blood ebbing back to her heart; then she said, in a distinct and level voice: "I know nothing of the history of Mr. Dawnish."

Lady Caroline gave a stare and a gasp. Her distracted hand groped for her boa and she began to wind it mechanically about her long neck.

"It would really be an enormous help to us—and to poor Gwendolen Matcher," she persisted pleadingly. "And you'd be doing Guy himself a good turn."

Margaret remained silent and motionless while her visitor drew on one of the worn gloves she had pulled off to adjust her veil. Lady Caroline gave the veil a final twitch.

"I've come a tremendously long way," she said, "and, since it isn't you, I can't think why you won't help me. . . ."

When the door had closed on her visitor Margaret Ransom went slowly up the stairs to her room. As she dragged her feet from one step to another, she remembered how she had sprung up the same steep flight after that visit of Guy Dawnish's when she had looked in the glass and seen on her face the blush of youth.

When she reached her room she bolted the door as she had done that day, and again looked at herself in the narrow mirror above her dressing-table. It was just a year since then—the elms were budding again, the willows hanging their green veil above the bench by the river. But there was no trace of youth left in her face—she saw it now as others had doubtless always seen it. If it seemed as it did to Lady Caroline Duckett, what look must it have worn to the fresh gaze of young Guy Dawnish?

A pretext—she had been a pretext. He had used her name to screen some one else—or perhaps merely to escape from a situation of which he was weary. She did not care to conjecture what his motive had been—everything connected with him had grown so remote and alien. She felt no anger—only an unspeakable sadness, a sadness which she knew would never be appeased.

She looked at herself long and steadily; she wished to clear her eyes of all illusions. Then she turned away and took her usual seat beside her work-table. From where she sat she could look down the empty elm-shaded street, up which, at this hour every day, she was sure to see her husband's figure advancing. She would see it presently—she would see it for many years to come. She had a sudden aching sense of the length of the years that stretched before her. Strange that one who was not young should still, in all likelihood, have so long to live!

Nothing was changed in the setting of her life, perhaps nothing would ever change in it. She would certainly live and die in Wentworth. And meanwhile the days would go on as usual, bringing the usual obligations. As the word flitted through her brain she remembered that she had still to put the finishing touches to the paper she was to read the next afternoon at the meeting of the Higher Thought Club.

The book she had been reading lay face downward beside her, where she had left it an hour ago. She took it up, and slowly and painfully, like a child laboriously spelling out the syllables, she went on with the rest of the sentence:

—"and they spring from a level not much above that of the springing of the transverse and diagonal ribs, which are so arranged as to give a convex curve to the surface of the vaulting conoid."

THE VERDICT

I HAD always thought Jack Gisburn rather a cheap genius—though a good fellow enough—so it was no great surprise to me to hear that, in the height of his glory, he had dropped his painting, married a rich widow, and established himself in a villa on the Riviera. (Though I rather thought it would have been Rome or Florence.)

"The height of his glory"—that was what the women called it. I can hear Mrs. Gideon Thwing—his last Chicago sitter—deploring his unaccountable abdication. "Of course it's going to send the value of my picture 'way up; but I don't think of that, Mr. Rickham—the loss to Arrt is all I think of." The word, on Mrs. Thwing's lips, multiplied its *rs* as though they were reflected in an endless vista of mirrors. And it was not only the Mrs. Thwings who mourned. Had not the exquisite Hermia Croft, at the last Grafton Gallery show, stopped me before Gisburn's "Moon-dancers" to say, with tears in her eyes: "We shall not look upon its like again"?

Well!—even through the prism of Hermia's tears I felt able to face the fact with equanimity. Poor Jack Gisburn! The women had made him—it was fitting that they should mourn him. Among his own sex fewer regrets were heard, and in his own trade hardly a murmur. Professional jealousy? Perhaps. If it were, the honour of the craft was vindicated by little Claude Nutley, who, in all good faith, brought out in the Burlington a very handsome "obituary" on Jack—one of those showy articles stocked with random technicalities that I have heard (I won't say by whom) compared to Gisburn's painting. And so—his resolve being apparently irrevocable—the discussion gradually died out, and, as Mrs. Thwing had predicted, the price of "Gisburns" went up.

It was not till three years later that, in the course of a few weeks' idling on the Riviera, it suddenly occurred to me to wonder why Gisburn had given up his painting. On reflection, it really was a tempting problem. To accuse his wife would have been too easy—his fair sitters had been denied the solace of saying that Mrs. Gisburn had "dragged him down." For Mrs. Gisburn—as such—had not existed till nearly a year after Jack's resolve had been taken. It might be that he had married her—since he liked his ease—because he didn't want to go on painting; but it would have been hard to prove that he had given up his painting because he had married her.

Of course, if she had not dragged him down, she had equally, as Miss Croft contended, failed to "lift him up"—she had not led him back to the easel. To put the brush into his hand again—what a vocation for a wife! But Mrs. Gisburn appeared to have disdained it—and I felt it might be interesting to find out why.

The desultory life of the Riviera lends itself to such purely academic speculations; and having, on my way to Monte Carlo, caught a glimpse of Jack's balustraded terraces between the pines, I had myself borne thither the next day.

I found the couple at tea beneath their palm-trees; and Mrs. Gisburn's welcome was so genial that, in the ensuing weeks, I claimed it frequently. It was not that my hostess was "interesting": on that point I could have given Miss Croft the fullest reassurance. It was just because she was *not* interesting—if I may be pardoned the bull—that I found her so. For Jack, all his life, had been surrounded by interesting women: they had fostered his art, it had been reared in the hot-house of their adulation. And it was therefore instructive to note what effect the "deadening atmosphere of mediocrity" (I quote Miss Croft) was having on him.

I have mentioned that Mrs. Gisburn was rich; and it was immediately perceptible that her husband was extracting from this circumstance a delicate but substantial satisfaction. It is, as a rule, the people who scorn money who get most out of it; and Jack's elegant disdain of his wife's big balance enabled him, with an appearance of perfect good-breeding, to transmute it into objects of art and luxury. To the latter, I must add, he remained relatively indifferent; but he was buying Renaissance bronzes and eighteenth-century pictures with a discrimination that bespoke the amplest resources.

"Money's only excuse is to put beauty into circulation," was one of the axioms he laid down across the Sevres and silver of an exquisitely appointed luncheon-table, when, on a later day, I had again run over from Monte Carlo; and Mrs. Gisburn, beaming on him, added for my enlightenment: "Jack is so morbidly sensitive to every form of beauty."

Poor Jack! It had always been his fate to have women say such things of him: the fact should be set down in extenuation. What struck me now was that, for the first time, he resented the tone. I had seen him, so often, basking under similar tributes—was it the conjugal note that robbed them of their savour? No—for, oddly enough, it became apparent that he was fond of Mrs. Gisburn—fond enough not to see her absurdity. It was his own absurdity he seemed to be wincing under—his own attitude as an object for garlands and incense.

"My dear, since I've chucked painting people don't say that stuff about me—they say it about Victor Grindle," was his only protest, as he rose from the table and strolled out onto the sunlit terrace.

I glanced after him, struck by his last word. Victor Grindle was, in fact, becoming the man of the moment—as Jack himself, one might put it, had been the man of the hour. The younger artist was said to have formed himself at my friend's feet, and I wondered if a tinge of jealousy underlay the latter's mysterious abdication. But no—for it was not till after that event that the *rose Dubarry* drawing-rooms had begun to display their "Grindles."

I turned to Mrs. Gisburn, who had lingered to give a lump of sugar to her spaniel in the dining-room.

"Why *has* he chucked painting?" I asked abruptly.

She raised her eyebrows with a hint of good-humoured surprise.

"Oh, he doesn't *have* to now, you know; and I want him to enjoy himself," she said quite simply.

I looked about the spacious white-panelled room, with its *famille-verte* vases repeating the tones of the pale damask curtains, and its eighteenth-century pastels in delicate faded frames.

"Has he chucked his pictures too? I haven't seen a single one in the house."

A slight shade of constraint crossed Mrs. Gisburn's open countenance. "It's his ridiculous modesty, you know. He says they're not fit to have about; he's sent them all away except one—my portrait—and that I have to keep upstairs."

His ridiculous modesty—Jack's modesty about his pictures? My curiosity was growing like the bean-stalk. I said persuasively to my hostess: "I must really see your portrait, you know."

She glanced out almost timorously at the terrace where her husband, lounging in a hooded chair, had lit a cigar and drawn the Russian deerhound's head between his knees.

"Well, come while he's not looking," she said, with a laugh that tried to hide her nervousness; and I followed her between the marble Emperors of the hall, and up the wide stairs with terra-cotta nymphs poised among flowers at each landing.

In the dimmest corner of her boudoir, amid a profusion of delicate and distinguished objects, hung one of the familiar oval canvases, in the inevitable garlanded frame. The mere outline of the frame called up all Gisburn's past!

Mrs. Gisburn drew back the window-curtains, moved aside a *jardiniere* full of pink azaleas, pushed an arm-chair away, and said: "If you stand here you can just manage to see it. I had it over the mantel-piece, but he wouldn't let it stay."

Yes—I could just manage to see it—the first portrait of Jack's I had ever had to strain my eyes over! Usually they had the place of honour—say the central panel in a pale yellow or *rose Dubarry* drawing-room, or a monumental easel placed so that it took the light through curtains of old Venetian point. The more modest place became the picture better; yet, as my eyes grew accustomed to the half-light, all the characteristic qualities came out—all the hesitations disguised as audacities, the tricks of prestidigitation by which, with such consummate skill, he managed to divert attention from the real business of the picture to some pretty irrelevance of detail. Mrs. Gisburn, presenting a neutral surface to work on—forming, as it were, so inevitably the background of her own picture—had lent herself in an unusual degree to the display of this false virtuosity. The picture was one of Jack's "strongest," as his admirers would have put it—it represented, on his part, a swelling of muscles, a congesting of veins, a balancing, straddling and straining, that reminded one of the circus-clown's ironic efforts to lift a feather. It met, in short, at every point the demand of lovely woman to be painted "strongly" because she was tired of being painted "sweetly"—and yet not to lose an atom of the sweetness.

"It's the last he painted, you know," Mrs. Gisburn said with pardonable pride. "The last but one," she corrected herself—"but the other doesn't count, because he destroyed it."

"Destroyed it?" I was about to follow up this clue when I heard a footstep and saw Jack himself on the threshold.

As he stood there, his hands in the pockets of his velveteen coat, the thin brown waves of hair pushed back from his white forehead, his lean sunburnt cheeks furrowed by a smile that lifted the tips of a self-confident moustache, I felt to what a degree he had the same quality as his pictures—the quality of looking cleverer than he was.

His wife glanced at him deprecatingly, but his eyes travelled past her to the portrait.

"Mr. Rickham wanted to see it," she began, as if excusing herself. He shrugged his shoulders, still smiling.

"Oh, Rickham found me out long ago," he said lightly; then, passing his arm through mine: "Come and see the rest of the house."

He showed it to me with a kind of naive suburban pride: the bathrooms, the speaking-tubes, the dress-closets, the trouser-presses—all the complex simplifications of the millionaire's domestic economy. And whenever my wonder paid the expected tribute he said, throwing out his chest a little: "Yes, I really don't see how people manage to live without that."

Well—it was just the end one might have foreseen for him. Only he was, through it all and in spite of it all—as he had been through, and in spite of, his pictures—so handsome, so charming, so disarming, that one longed to cry out: "Be dissatisfied with your leisure!" as once one had longed to say: "Be dissatisfied with your work!"

But, with the cry on my lips, my diagnosis suffered an unexpected check.

"This is my own lair," he said, leading me into a dark plain room at the end of the florid vista. It was square and brown and leathery: no "effects"; no bric-a-brac, none of the air of posing for reproduction in a picture weekly—above all, no least sign of ever having been used as a studio.

The fact brought home to me the absolute finality of Jack's break with his old life.

"Don't you ever dabble with paint any more?" I asked, still looking about for a trace of such activity.

"Never," he said briefly.

"Or water-colour—or etching?"

His confident eyes grew dim, and his cheeks paled a little under their handsome sunburn.

"Never think of it, my dear fellow—any more than if I'd never touched a brush."

And his tone told me in a flash that he never thought of anything else.

I moved away, instinctively embarrassed by my unexpected discovery; and as I turned, my eye fell on a small picture above the mantelpiece—the only object breaking the plain oak panelling of the room.

"Oh, by Jove!" I said.

It was a sketch of a donkey—an old tired donkey, standing in the rain under a wall.

"By Jove—a Stroud!" I cried.

He was silent; but I felt him close behind me, breathing a little quickly.

"What a wonder! Made with a dozen lines—but on everlasting foundations. You lucky chap, where did you get it?"

He answered slowly: "Mrs. Stroud gave it to me."

"Ah—I didn't know you even knew the Strouds. He was such an inflexible hermit."

"I didn't—till after. . . . She sent for me to paint him when he was dead."

"When he was dead? You?"

I must have let a little too much amazement escape through my surprise, for he answered with a deprecating laugh: "Yes—she's an awful simpleton, you know, Mrs. Stroud. Her only idea was to have him done by a fashionable painter—ah, poor Stroud! She thought it the surest way of proclaiming his greatness—of forcing it on a purblind public. And at the moment I was *the* fashionable painter."

"Ah, poor Stroud—as you say. Was *that* his history?"

"That was his history. She believed in him, gloried in him—or thought she did. But she couldn't bear not to have all the drawing-rooms with her. She couldn't bear the fact that, on varnishing days, one could always get near enough to see his pictures. Poor woman! She's just a fragment groping for other fragments. Stroud is the only whole I ever knew."

"You ever knew? But you just said—"

Gisburn had a curious smile in his eyes.

"Oh, I knew him, and he knew me—only it happened after he was dead."

I dropped my voice instinctively. "When she sent for you?"

"Yes—quite insensible to the irony. She wanted him vindicated—and by me!"

He laughed again, and threw back his head to look up at the sketch of the donkey. "There were days when I couldn't look at that thing—couldn't face it. But I forced myself to put it here; and now it's cured me—cured me. That's the reason why I don't dabble any more, my dear Rickham; or rather Stroud himself is the reason."

For the first time my idle curiosity about my companion turned into a serious desire to understand him better.

"I wish you'd tell me how it happened," I said.

He stood looking up at the sketch, and twirling between his fingers a cigarette he had forgotten to light. Suddenly he turned toward me.

"I'd rather like to tell you—because I've always suspected you of loathing my work."

I made a deprecating gesture, which he negatived with a good-humoured shrug.

"Oh, I didn't care a straw when I believed in myself—and now it's an added tie between us!"

He laughed slightly, without bitterness, and pushed one of the deep arm-chairs forward. "There: make yourself comfortable—and here are the cigars you like."

He placed them at my elbow and continued to wander up and down the room, stopping now and then beneath the picture.

"How it happened? I can tell you in five minutes—and it didn't take much longer to happen. . . . I can remember now how surprised and pleased I was when I got Mrs. Stroud's note. Of course, deep down, I had always *felt* there was no one like him—only I had gone with the stream, echoed the usual platitudes about him, till I half got to think he was a failure, one of the kind that are left behind. By Jove, and he *was* left behind—because he had come to stay! The rest of us had to let ourselves be swept along or go under, but he was high above the current—on everlasting foundations, as you say.

"Well, I went off to the house in my most egregious mood—rather moved, Lord forgive me, at the pathos of poor Stroud's career of failure being crowned by the glory of my painting him! Of course I meant to do the picture for nothing—I told Mrs. Stroud so when she began to stammer something about her poverty. I remember getting off a prodigious phrase about the honour being *mine*—oh, I was princely, my dear Rickham! I was posing to myself like one of my own sitters.

"Then I was taken up and left alone with him. I had sent all my traps in advance, and I had only to set up the easel and get to work. He had been dead only twenty-four hours, and he died suddenly, of heart disease, so that there had been no preliminary work of destruction—his face was clear and untouched. I had met him once or twice, years before, and thought him insignificant and dingy. Now I saw that he was superb.

"I was glad at first, with a merely aesthetic satisfaction: glad to have my hand on such a 'subject.' Then his strange life-likeness began to affect me queerly—as I blocked the head in I felt as if he were watching me do it. The sensation was followed by the thought: if he *were* watching me, what would he say to my way of working? My strokes began to go a little wild—I felt nervous and uncertain.

"Once, when I looked up, I seemed to see a smile behind his close grayish beard—as if he had the secret, and were amusing himself by holding it back from me. That exasperated me still more. The secret? Why, I had a secret worth twenty of his! I dashed at the canvas furiously, and tried some of my bravura tricks. But they failed me, they crumbled. I saw that he wasn't watching the showy bits—I couldn't distract his attention; he just kept his eyes on the hard passages between. Those were the ones I had always shirked, or covered up with some lying paint. And how he saw through my lies!

"I looked up again, and caught sight of that sketch of the donkey hanging on the wall near his bed. His wife told me afterward it was the last thing he had done—just a note taken with a shaking hand, when he was down in Devonshire recovering from a previous heart attack. Just a note! But it tells his whole history. There are years of patient scornful persistence in every line. A man who had swum with the current could never have learned that mighty up-stream stroke. . . .

"I turned back to my work, and went on groping and muddling; then I looked at the donkey again. I saw that, when Stroud laid in the first stroke, he knew just what the end would be. He had possessed his subject, absorbed it, recreated it. When had I done that with any of my things? They hadn't been born of me—I had just adopted them. . . .

"Hang it, Rickham, with that face watching me I couldn't do another stroke. The plain truth was, I didn't know where to put it—*I had never known*. Only, with my sitters and my public, a showy splash of colour covered up the fact—I just threw paint into their faces. . . . Well, paint was the one medium those dead eyes could see through—see straight to the tottering foundations underneath. Don't you know how, in talking a foreign language, even fluently, one says half the time not what one wants to but what one can? Well—that was the way I painted; and as he lay there and watched me, the thing they called my 'technique' collapsed like a house of cards. He didn't sneer, you understand, poor Stroud—he just lay there quietly watching, and on his lips, through the gray beard, I seemed to hear the question: 'Are you sure you know where you're coming out?'

"If I could have painted that face, with that question on it, I should have done a great thing. The next greatest thing was to see that I couldn't—and that grace was given me. But, oh, at that minute, Rickham, was there anything on earth I wouldn't have given to have

Stroud alive before me, and to hear him say: 'It's not too late—I'll show you how'?

"It *was* too late—it would have been, even if he'd been alive. I packed up my traps, and went down and told Mrs. Stroud. Of course I didn't tell her *that*—it would have been Greek to her. I simply said I couldn't paint him, that I was too moved. She rather liked the idea—she's so romantic! It was that that made her give me the donkey. But she was terribly upset at not getting the portrait—she did so want him 'done' by some one showy! At first I was afraid she wouldn't let me off—and at my wits' end I suggested Grindle. Yes, it was I who started Grindle: I told Mrs. Stroud he was the 'coming' man, and she told somebody else, and so it got to be true. . . . And he painted Stroud without wincing; and she hung the picture among her husband's things. . . ."

He flung himself down in the arm-chair near mine, laid back his head, and clasping his arms beneath it, looked up at the picture above the chimney-piece.

"I like to fancy that Stroud himself would have given it to me, if he'd been able to say what he thought that day."

And, in answer to a question I put half-mechanically—"Begin again?" he flashed out. "When the one thing that brings me anywhere near him is that I knew enough to leave off?"

He stood up and laid his hand on my shoulder with a laugh. "Only the irony of it is that I *am* still painting—since Grindle's doing it for me! The Strouds stand alone, and happen once—but there's no exterminating our kind of art."

THE POT-BOILER

I

THE studio faced north, looking out over a dismal reach of roofs and chimneys, and rusty fire-escapes hung with heterogeneous garments. A crust of dirty snow covered the level surfaces, and a December sky with more snow in it lowered over them.

The room was bare and gaunt, with blotched walls and a stained uneven floor. On a divan lay a pile of "properties"—limp draperies, an Algerian scarf, a moth-eaten fan of peacock feathers. The janitor had forgotten to fill the coal-scuttle over-night, and the cast-iron stove projected its cold flanks into the room like a black iceberg. Ned Stanwell, who had just added his hat and great-coat to the miscellaneous heap on the divan, turned from the empty stove with a shiver.

"By Jove, this is a little too much like the last act of *Boheme*," he said, slipping into his coat again after a vain glance at the coal-scuttle. Much solitude, and a lively habit of mind, had bred in him the habit of audible soliloquy, and having flung a shout for the janitor down the seven flights dividing the studio from the basement, he turned back, picking up the thread of his monologue. "Exactly like *Boheme*, really—that crack in the wall is much more like a stage-crack than a real one—just the sort of crack Mungold would paint if he were doing a Humble Interior."

Mungold, the fashionable portrait-painter of the hour, was the favourite object of the younger men's irony.

"It only needs Kate Arran to be borne in dying," Stanwell continued with a laugh. "Much more likely to be poor little Caspar, though," he concluded.

His neighbour across the landing—the little sculptor, Caspar Arran, humorously called "Gasper" on account of his bronchial asthma—had lately been joined by a sister, Kate Arran, a strapping girl, fresh from the country, who had installed herself in the little room off her brother's studio, keeping house for him with a chafing-dish and a coffee-machine, to the mirth and envy of the other young men in the building.

Poor little Gasper had been very bad all the autumn, and it was surmised that his sister's presence, which he spoke of growlingly, as a troublesome necessity devolved on him by the inopportune death of an aunt, was really an indication of his failing ability to take care of himself. Kate Arran took his complaints with unfailing good-humour, darned his socks, brushed his clothes, fed him with steaming broths and foaming milk-punches, and listened with reverential assent to his interminable disquisitions on art. Every one in the house was sorry for little Gasper, and the other fellows liked him all the more because it was so impossible to like his sculpture; but his talk was a bore, and when his colleagues ran in to see him they were apt to keep a hand on the door-knob and to plead a pressing engagement. At least they had been till Kate came; but now they began to show a disposition to enter and sit down. Caspar, who was no fool, perceived the change, and perhaps detected its cause; at any rate, he showed no special gratification at the increased cordiality of his friends, and Kate, who followed him in everything, took this as a sign that guests were to be discouraged.

There was one exception, however: Ned Stanwell, who was deplorably good-natured, had always lent a patient ear to Caspar, and he now reaped his reward by being taken into Kate's favour. Before she had been a month in the building they were on confidential terms as to Caspar's health, and lately Stanwell had penetrated farther, even to the inmost recesses of her anxiety about her brother's career. Caspar had recently had a bad blow in the refusal of his *magnum opus*—a vast allegorical group—by the Commissioners of the Minneapolis Exhibition. He took the rejection with Promethean irony, proclaimed it as the clinching proof of his ability, and abounded in reasons why, even in an age of such crass artistic ignorance, a refusal so egregious must react to the advantage of its object. But his sister's indignation, if as glowing, was a shade less hopeful. Of course Caspar was going to succeed—she knew it was only a question of time—but she paled at the word and turned imploring eyes on Stanwell. *Was there time enough?* It was the one element in the combination that she could not count on; and Stanwell, reddening under her look of interrogation, and cursing his own glaring robustness, would affirm that of course, of course, of course, by everything that was holy there was time enough—with the mental reservation that there wouldn't be, even if poor Caspar lived to be a hundred.

"Vos that you yelling for the shanitor, Mr. Sdanwell?" inquired an affable voice through the doorway; and Stanwell, turning with a laugh, confronted the squat figure of a middle-aged man in an expensive fur coat, who looked as if his face secreted the oil which he used on his hair.

"Hullo, Shepson—I should say I was yelling. Did you ever feel such an atmosphere? That fool has forgotten to light the stove. Come in, but for heaven's sake don't take off your coat."

Mr. Shepson glanced about the studio with a look which seemed to say that, where so much else was lacking, the absence of a fire hardly added to the general sense of destitution.

"Vell, you ain't as vell fixed as Mr. Mungold—ever been to his studio, Mr. Sdanwell? De most ex*quis*ite blush hangings, and a gas-fire, choost as natural—"

"Oh, hang it, Shepson, do you call *that* a studio? It's like a manicure's parlour—or a beauty-doctor's. By George," broke off Stanwell, "and that's just what he is!"

"A peauty-doctor?"

"Yes—oh, well, you wouldn't see," murmured Stanwell, mentally storing his epigram for more appreciative ears. "But you didn't come just to make me envious of Mungold's studio, did you?" And he pushed forward a chair for his visitor.

The latter, however, declined it with an affable motion. "Of gourse not, of gourse not—but Mr. Mungold is a sensible man. He makes a lot of money, you know."

"Is that what you came to tell me?" said Stanwell, still humorously.

"My gootness, no—I was downstairs looking at Holbrook's sdained class, and I shoost thought I'd sdep up a minute and take a beep at your vork."

"Much obliged, I'm sure—especially as I assume that you don't want any of it." Try as he would, Stanwell could not keep a note of eagerness from his voice. Mr. Shepson caught the note, and eyed him shrewdly through gold-rimmed glasses.

"Vell, vell, vell—I'm not prepared to commit myself. Shoost let me take a look round, vill you?"

"With the greatest pleasure—and I'll give another shout for the coal."

Stanwell went out on the landing, and Mr. Shepson, left to himself, began a meditative progress about the room. On an easel facing the improvised dais stood a canvas on which a young woman's head had been blocked in. It was just in that happy state of semi-evocation when a picture seems to detach itself from the grossness of its medium and live a wondrous moment in the actual; and the quality of the head in question—a vigorous dusky youthfulness, a kind of virgin majesty—lent itself to this illusion of vitality. Stanwell, who had re-entered the studio, could not help drawing a sharp breath as he saw the picture-dealer pausing with tilted head before this portrait: it seemed, at one moment, so impossible that he should not be struck with it, at the next so incredible that he should be.

Shepson cocked his parrot-eye at the canvas with a desultory "Vat's dat?" which sent a twinge through the young man.

"That? Oh—a sketch of a young lady," stammered Stanwell, flushing at the imbecility of his reply. "It's Miss Arran, you know," he added, "the sister of my neighbour here, the sculptor."

"Sgulpture? There's no market for modern sgulpture except tombstones," said Shepson disparagingly, passing on as if he included the sister's portrait in his condemnation of her brother's trade.

Stanwell smiled, but more at himself than Shepson. How could he ever have supposed that the gross fool would see anything in his sketch of Kate Arran? He stood aside, straining after detachment, while the dealer continued his round of exploration, waddling up to the canvases on the walls, prodding with his stick at those stacked in corners, prying and peering sideways like a great bird rummaging for seed. He seemed to find little nutriment in the course of his search, for the sounds he emitted expressed a weary distaste for misdirected effort, and he completed his round without having thought it worth while to draw a single canvas from its obscurity.

As his visits always had the same result, Stanwell was reduced to wondering why he had come again; but Shepson was not the man to indulge in vague roamings through the field of art, and it was safe to conclude that his purpose would in due course reveal itself. His tour brought him at length face to face with the painter, where he paused, clasping his plump gloved hands behind his back, and shaking an admonitory head.

"Gleffer—very gleffer, of course—I suppose you'll let me know when you want to sell anything?"

"Let you know?" gasped Stanwell, to whom the room grew so glowingly hot that he thought for a moment the janitor must have made up the fire.

Shepson gave a dry laugh. "Vell, it doesn't sdrike me that you want to now—doing this kind of thing, you know!" And he swept a comprehensive hand about the studio.

"Ah," said Stanwell, who could not keep a note of flatness out of his laugh.

"See here, Mr. Sdanwell, vot do you do it for? If you do it for yourself and the other fellows, vell and good—only don't ask me round. I sell pictures, I don't theorize about them. Ven you vant to sell, gome to me with what my gustomers vant. You can do it—you're smart enough. You can do most anything. Vere's dat bortrait of Gladys Glyde dat you showed at the Fake Club last autumn? Dat little thing in de Romney sdyle? Dat vas a little shem, now," exclaimed Mr. Shepson, whose pronunciation became increasingly Semitic in moments of excitement.

Stanwell stared. Called upon a few months previously to contribute to an exhibition of skits on well-known artists, he had used the photograph of a favourite music-hall "star" as the basis of a picture in the pseudo-historical style affected by the popular portrait-painters of the day.

"That thing?" he said contemptuously. "How on earth did you happen to see it?"

"I see everything," returned the dealer with an oracular smile. "If you've got it here let me look at it, please."

It cost Stanwell a few minutes' search to unearth his skit—a clever blending of dash and sentimentality, in just the right proportion to create the impression of a powerful brush subdued to mildness by the charms of the sitter. Stanwell had thrown it off in a burst of imitative frenzy, beginning for the mere joy of the satire, but gradually fascinated by the problem of producing the requisite mingling of attributes. He was surprised now to see how well he had caught the note, and Shepson's face reflected his approval.

"By George! Dat's something like," the dealer ejaculated.

"Like what? Like Mungold?" Stanwell laughed.

"Like business! Like a big order for a bortrait, Mr. Sdanwell—dat's what it's like!" cried Shepson, swinging round on him.

Stanwell's stare widened. "An order for me?"

"Vy not? Accidents *vill* happen," said Shepson jocosely. "De fact is, Mrs. Archer Millington wants to be bainted—you know her sdyle? Well, she prides herself on her likeness to little Gladys. And so ven she saw dat bicture of yours at de Fake Show she made a note of your name, and de udder day she sent for me and she says: 'Mr. Shepson,

I'm tired of Mungold—all my friends are done by Mungold. I vant to break away and be orishinal—I vant to be done by the bainter that did Gladys Glyde.'"

Shepson waited to observe the result of this overwhelming announcement, and Stanwell, after a momentary halt of surprise, brought out laughingly: "But this *is* a Mungold. Is this what she calls being original?"

"Shoost exactly," said Shepson, with unexpected acuteness. "That's vat dey all want—something different from what all deir friends have got, but shoost like it all de same. Dat's de public all over! Mrs. Millington don't want a Mungold, because everybody's got a Mungold, but she wants a picture that's in the same sdyle, because dat's *de* sdyle, and she's afraid of any oder!"

Stanwell was listening with real enjoyment. "Ah, you know your public," he murmured.

"Vell, you do, too, or you couldn't have painted dat," the dealer retorted. "And I don't say dey're wrong—mind dat. I like a bretty picture myself. And I understand the way dey feel. Dey're villing to let Sargent take liberties vid them, because it's like being punched in de ribs by a King; but if anybody else baints them, they vant to look as sweet as an obituary." He turned earnestly to Stanwell. "The thing is to attract their notice. Vonce you got it they von't gif you dime to sleep. And dat's why I'm here to-day—you've attracted Mrs. Millington's notice, and vonce you're hung in dat new ball-room—dat's vere she vants you, in a big gold panel—vonce you're dere, vy, you'll be like the Pianola—no home gompleat without you. And I ain't going to charge you any commission on the first job!"

He stood before the painter, exuding a mixture of deference and patronage in which either element might predominate as events developed; but Stanwell could see in the incident only the stuff for a good story.

"My dear Shepson," he said, "what are you talking about? This is no picture of mine. Why don't you ask me to do you a Corot at once? I hear there's a great demand for them still in the West. Or an Arthur Schracker—I can do Schracker as well as Mungold," he added, turning around a small canvas at which a paint-pot seemed to have been hurled with violence from a considerable distance.

Shepson ignored the allusion to Corot, but screwed his eyes at the picture. "Ah, Schracker—vell, the Schracker sdyle would take first rate if you were a foreigner—but, for goodness sake, don't try it on Mrs. Millington!"

Stanwell pushed the two skits aside. "Oh, you can trust me," he cried humorously. "The pearls and the eyes very large—the extremities very small. Isn't that about the size of it?"

Dat's it—dat's it. And the cheque as big as you vant to make it! Mrs. Millington vants the picture finished in time for her first barty in the new ball-room, and if you rush the job she won't sdickle at an extra thousand. Vill you come along with me now and arrange for your first sitting?"

He stood before the young man, urgent, paternal, and so imbued with the importance of his mission that his face stretched to a ludicrous length of dismay when Stanwell, administering a good-humoured push to his shoulder, cried gaily: "My dear fellow, it will make my price rise still higher when the lady hears I'm too busy to take any orders at present—and that I'm actually obliged to turn you out now because I'm expecting a sitter!"

It was part of Shepson's business to have a quick ear for the note of finality, and he offered no resistance to Stanwell's friendly impulsion; but on the threshold he paused to murmur, with a regretful glance at the denuded studio: "You could haf done it, Mr. Sdanwell—you could haf done it!"

II

KATE ARRAN was Stanwell's sitter; but the janitor had hardly filled the stove when she came in to say that she could not sit. Caspar had had a bad night: he was depressed and feverish, and in spite of his protests she had resolved to fetch the doctor. Care sat on her usually tranquil features, and Stanwell, as he offered to go for the doctor, wished he could have caught in his picture the wide gloom of her brow. There was always a kind of Biblical breadth in the expression of her emotions, and today she suggested a text from Isaiah.

"But you're not busy?" she hesitated; in the full voice which seemed tuned to a solemn rhetoric.

"I meant to be—with you. But since that's off I'm quite unemployed."

She smiled interrogatively. "I thought perhaps you had an order. I met Mr. Shepson rubbing his hands on the landing."

"Was he rubbing his hands? Well, it was not over me. He says that from the style of my pictures he doesn't suppose I want to sell."

She looked at him superbly. "Well, do you?"

He embraced his bleak walls in a circular gesture. "Judge for yourself!"

"Ah, but it's splendidly furnished!"

"With rejected pictures, you mean?"

"With ideals!" she exclaimed in a tone caught from her brother, and which would have been irritating to Stanwell if it had not been moving.

He gave a slight shrug and took up his hat; but she interposed to say that if it didn't make any difference she would prefer to have him go and sit with poor Caspar, while she ran for the doctor and did some household errands by the way. Stanwell divined in her request the need for a brief respite from Caspar, and though he shivered at the thought of her facing the cold in the scant jacket which had been her only wear since he had known her, he let her go without a protest, and betook himself to Arran's studio.

He found the little sculptor dressed and roaming fretfully about the melancholy room in which he and his plastic off-spring lodged together. In one corner, where Kate's chair and work-table stood, a scrupulous order prevailed; but the rest of the apartment had the dreary untidiness, the damp grey look, which the worker in clay usually creates about him. In the centre of this desert stood the shrouded image of Caspar's disappointment: the colossal rejected group as to which his friends could seldom remember whether it represented Jove hurling a Titan from Olympus or Science Subjugating Religion. Caspar was the sworn foe of religion, which he appeared to regard as indirectly connected with his inability to sell his statues.

The sculptor was too ill to work, and Stanwell's appearance loosed the pent-up springs of his talk.

"Hullo! What are you doing here? I thought Kate had gone over to sit to you. She wanted a little fresh air? I should say enough of it came in through these windows. How like a woman, when she's agreed to do a certain thing, to make up her mind at once that she's got to do another! They don't call it caprice—it's always duty: that's the humour of it. I'll be bound Kate alleged a pressing engagement. Sorry she should waste your time so, my dear fellow. Here am I with plenty of it to burn—look at my hand shake; I can't do a thing! Well, luckily nobody wants me to—posterity may suffer, but the present generation isn't worrying. The present generation wants to be carved in sugar-candy, or painted in maple syrup. It doesn't want to be told the truth about itself or about anything in the universe. The prophets have always lived in a garret, my dear fellow—only the ravens don't always find out their address! Speaking of ravens, though, Kate told me she saw old Shepson coming out of your place—I say, old man, you're not meditating an apostasy? You're not doing the kind of thing that Shepson would look at?"

Stanwell laughed. "Oh, he looked at them—but only to confirm his reasons for rejecting them."

"Ha! ha! That's right—he wanted to refresh his memory with their badness. But how on earth did he happen to have any doubts on the subject? I should as soon have thought of his coming in here!"

Stanwell winced at the analogy, but replied in Caspar's key: "Oh, he's not as sure of any of us as he is of you!"

The sculptor received this tribute with a joyous expletive. "By God, no, he's sure of me, as you say! He and his tribe know that I'll starve in my tracks sooner than make a concession—a single concession. A fellow came after me once to do an angel on a tombstone—an angel leaning against a broken column, and looking as if it was waiting for the elevator and wondering why in hell it didn't come. He said he wanted me to show that the deceased was pining to get to heaven. As she was his wife I didn't dispute the proposition, but when I asked him what he understood by *heaven* he grabbed his hat and walked out of the studio. *He* didn't wait for the elevator."

Stanwell listened with a practised smile. The story of the man who had come to order the angel was so familiar to Arran's friends that its only interest consisted in waiting to see what variation he would give to the retort which had put the mourner to flight. It was generally supposed that this visit represented the sculptor's nearest approach to an order, and one of his fellow-craftsmen had been heard to remark that if Caspar *had* made the tombstone, the lady under it would have tried harder than ever to get to heaven. To Stanwell's present mood, however, there was something more than usually irritating in the gratuitous assumption that Arran had only to derogate from his altitude to have a press of purchasers at his door.

"Well—what did you gain by kicking your widower out?" he objected. "Why can't a man do two kinds of work—one to please himself and the other to boil the pot?"

Caspar stopped in his jerky walk—the stride of a tall man attempted with short legs (it sometimes appeared to Stanwell to symbolize his artistic endeavour).

"Why can't a man—why can't he? You ask me that, Stanwell?" he blazed out.

"Yes; and what's more, I'll answer you: it isn't everybody who can adapt his art as he wants to!"

Caspar stood before him, gasping with incredulous scorn. "Adapt his art? As he wants to? Unhappy wretch, what lingo are you talking? If you mean that it isn't every honest man who can be a renegade—"

"That's just what I do mean: he can't unless he's clever enough to see the other side."

The deep groan with which Caspar met this casuistry was cut short by a knock at the studio door, which thereupon opened to admit a small dapperly-dressed man with a silky moustache and mildly-bulging eyes.

"Ah, Mungold," exclaimed Stanwell, to cover the gloomy silence with which Arran received the new-comer; whereat the latter, with the air of a man who does not easily believe himself unwelcome, bestowed a sympathetic pressure on the sculptor's hand.

"My dear chap, I've just met Miss Arran, and she told me you were laid up with a bad cold, so I thought I'd pop in and cheer you up a little."

He looked about him with a smile evidently intended as the first act in his beneficent programme.

Mr. Mungold, freshly soaped and scented, with a neat glaze of gentility extending from his varnished boot-tips to his glossy hat, looked like the "flattered" portrait of a common man—just such an idealized presentment as his own brush might have produced. As a rule, however, he devoted himself to the portrayal of the other sex, painting ladies in syrup, as Arran said, with marsh-mallow children leaning against their knees. He was as quick as a dressmaker at catching new ideas, and the style of his pictures changed as rapidly as that of the fashion-plates. One year all his sitters were done on oval canvases, with gauzy draperies and a background of clouds; the next they were seated under an immemorial elm, caressing enormous dogs obviously constructed out of door-mats. Whatever their occupation they always looked straight out of the canvas, giving the impression that their eyes were fixed on an invisible camera. This gave rise to the rumour that Mungold "did" his portraits from photographs; it was even said that he had invented a way of transferring an enlarged photograph to the canvas, so that all that remained was to fill in the colours. If he heard of this charge he took it calmly, but probably it had not reached the high spheres in which he moved, and in which he was esteemed for painting pearls better, and making unsuggestive children look lovelier, than any of his fellow-craftsmen. Mr. Mungold, in fact, deemed it a part of his professional duty to study his sitters in their home-life; and as this life was chiefly led in the homes of others, he was too busy dining out and going to the opera to mingle much with his colleagues. But as no one is wholly consistent, Mr. Mungold had lately belied his ambitions by falling in love with Kate Arran; and with that gentle persistency which made him so wonderful in managing obstreperous infantile sitters, he had contrived to establish a precarious footing in her brother's studio.

Part of his success was due to the fact that he could not easily think himself the object of a rebuff. If it seemed to hit him he regarded it as deflected from its aim, and brushed it aside with a discreet gesture. A touch of comedy was lent to the situation by the fact that, till Kate Arran's coming, Mungold had always served as her brother's Awful Example. It was a mark of Arran's lack of humour that he persisted in regarding the little man as a conscious apostate, instead of perceiving that he painted as he could, in a world which really looked to him like a vast confectioner's window. Stanwell had never quite divined how Mungold had won over the sister, to whom her brother's prejudices were a religion; but he suspected the painter of having united a deep belief in Caspar's gifts with the occasional offer of opportune delicacies—the port-wine or game which Kate had no other means of procuring for her patient.

Stanwell, persuaded that Mungold would stick to his post till Miss Arran's return, felt himself freed from his promise to the latter and left the incongruous pair to themselves. There had been a time when it amused him to see Caspar submerge the painter in a torrent of turbid eloquence, and to watch poor Mungold sputtering under the rush of denunciation, yet emitting little bland phrases of assent, like a gentleman drowning correctly, in gloves and eye-glasses. But Stanwell was beginning to find less food for gaiety than for envy in the contemplation of his colleague. After all, Mungold held his ground, he did not go under. Spite of his manifest absurdity he had succeeded in propitiating the sister, in making himself tolerated by the brother; and the fact that his success was due to the ability to purchase port-wine and game was not in this case a mitigating circumstance. Stanwell knew that the Arrans really preferred him to Mungold, but the knowledge only sharpened his envy of the latter, whose friendship could command visible tokens of expression, while poor Stanwell's remained gloomily inarticulate. As he returned to his over-populated studio and surveyed anew the pictures of which

Shepson had not offered to relieve him, he found himself wishing, not for Mungold's lack of scruples, for he believed him to be the most scrupulous of men, but for that happy mean of talent which so completely satisfied the artistic requirements of the inartistic. Mungold was not to be despised as an apostate—he was to be congratulated as a man whose aptitudes were exactly in line with the taste of the persons he liked to dine with.

At this point in his meditations, Stanwell's eye fell on the portrait of Miss Gladys Glyde. It was really, as Shepson said, as good as a Mungold; yet it could never be made to serve the same purpose, because it was the work of a man who knew it was bad art. That at least would have been Caspar Arran's contention—poor Caspar, who produced as bad art in the service of the loftiest convictions! The distinction began to look like mere casuistry to Stanwell. He had never been very proud of his own adaptability. It had seemed to him to indicate the lack of an individual stand-point, and he had tried to counteract it by the cultivation of an aggressively personal style. But the cursed knack was in his fingers—he was always at the mercy of some other man's sensations, and there were moments when he blushed to remember that his grandfather had spent a laborious life-time in Rome, copying the Old Masters for a generation which lacked the facile resource of the camera. Now, however, it struck him that the ancestral versatility might be a useful inheritance. In art, after all, the greatest of them did what they could; and if a man could do several things instead of one, why should he not profit by the multiplicity of his gifts? If one had two talents why not serve two masters?

III

STANWELL, while seeing Caspar through the attack which had been the cause of his sister's arrival, had struck up a friendship with the young doctor who climbed the patient's seven flights with unremitting fidelity. The two, since then, had continued to exchange confidences regarding the sculptor's health, and Stanwell, anxious to waylay the doctor after his visit, left the studio door ajar, and went out when he heard a sound of leave-taking across the landing. But it appeared that the doctor had just come, and that it was Mungold who was making his adieux.

The latter at once assumed that Stanwell had been on the alert for him, and met the supposed advance by affably inviting himself into the studio.

"May I come and take a look around, my dear fellow? I have been meaning to drop in for an age—" Mungold always spoke with a girlish emphasis and effusiveness—"but I have been so busy getting up Mrs. Van Orley's tableaux—English eighteenth century portraits, you know—that really, what with that and my sittings, I've hardly had time to think. And then you know you owe me about a dozen visits! But you're a savage—you don't pay visits. You stay here and *piocher*—which is wiser, as the results prove. Ah, you're very strong—immensely strong!" He paused in the middle of the studio, glancing about a little apprehensively, as though he thought the stored energy of the pictures might result in an explosion. "Very original—very striking—ah, Miss Arran! A powerful head; but—excuse the suggestion—isn't there just the least little lack of sweetness? You don't think she has the sweet type? Perhaps not—but could she be so lovely if she were not intensely feminine? Just at present, though, she is not looking her best—she is horribly tired. I am afraid there is very little money left—and poor dear Caspar is so impossible: he won't hear of a loan. Otherwise I should be most happy—. But I came just now to propose a piece of work—in fact to give him an order. Mrs. Archer Millington has built a new ballroom, as I daresay you may have seen in the papers, and she has been kind enough to ask me for some hints—oh, merely as a friend: I don't presume to do more than advise. But her decorator wants to do something with Cupids—something light and playful, you understand. And so I ventured to say that I knew a very clever sculptor—well, I *do* believe Caspar has talent—latent talent, you know—and at any rate a job of that sort would be a big lift for him. At least I thought he would regard it so; but you should have heard him when I showed him the decorator's sketch. He asked me what the Cupids were to be done in—lard? And if I thought he had had his training at a confectioner's? And I don't know what more besides—but he worked himself up to such a degree that he brought on a frightful fit of coughing, and Miss Arran, I'm afraid, was rather annoyed with me when she came in, though I'm sure an order from Mrs. Archer Millington is not a thing that would annoy most people!"

Mr. Mungold paused, breathless with the rehearsal of his wrongs, and Stanwell said with a smile: "You know poor Caspar is terribly stiff on the purity of the artist's aim."

"The artist's aim?" Mr. Mungold stared. "What is the artist's aim but to please—isn't that the purpose of all true art? But his theories are so extravagant. I really don't know what I shall say to Mrs. Millington—she is not used to being refused. I suppose I had better put it on the ground of ill-health." The artist glanced at his handsome repeater. "Dear me, I promised to be at Mrs. Van Orley's before twelve o'clock. We are to settle about the curtain before luncheon. My dear fellow, it has been a privilege to see your work. By the way, you have never done any modelling, I suppose? You're so extraordinarily versatile—I didn't know whether you might care to undertake the Cupids yourself."

Stanwell had to wait a long time for the doctor; and when the latter came out he looked grave. Worse? No, he couldn't say that Caspar was worse—but then he wasn't any better. There was nothing mortal the matter, but the question was how long he could hold out. It was the kind of case where there is no use in drugs—he had just scribbled a prescription to quiet Miss Arran.

"It's the cold, I suppose," Stanwell groaned. "He ought to be shipped off to Florida."

The doctor made a negative gesture. "Florida be hanged! What he wants is to sell his group. That would set him up quicker than sitting on the equator."

"Sell his group?" Stanwell echoed. "But he's so indifferent to recognition—he believes in himself so thoroughly. I thought at first he would be hard hit when the Exhibition Committee refused it, but he seems to regard that as another proof of its superiority."

His visitor turned on him the penetrating eye of the confessor. "Indifferent to recognition? He's eating his heart out for it. Can't you see that all that talk is just so much whistling to keep his courage up? The name of his disease is failure—and I can't write the prescription that will cure that complaint. But if somebody would come along and take a fancy to those two naked parties who are breaking each other's heads, we'd have Mr. Caspar putting on a pound a day."

The truth of this diagnosis became suddenly vivid to Stanwell. How dull of him not to have seen before that it was not cold or privation which was killing Caspar—not anxiety for his sister's future, nor the ache of watching her daily struggle—but simply the cankering thought that he might die before he had made himself known! It was his vanity that was starving to death, and all Mungold's hampers could not appease that hunger. Stanwell was not shocked by the discovery—he was only the more sorry for the little man, who was, after all, denied that solace of self-sufficiency which his talk so noisily proclaimed. His lot seemed hard enough when Stanwell had pictured him as buoyed up by the scorn of public opinion—it became tragic if he was denied that support. The artist wondered if Kate had guessed her brother's secret, or if she were still the dupe of his stoicism. Stanwell was sure that the sculptor would take no one into his confidence, and least of all his sister, whose faith in his artistic independence was the chief prop of that tottering pose. Kate's penetration was not great, and Stanwell recalled the incredulous smile with which she had heard him defend poor Mungold's "sincerity" against Caspar's assaults; but she had the insight of the heart, and where her brother's happiness was concerned she might have seen deeper than any of them. It was this last consideration which took the strongest hold on Stanwell—he felt Caspar's sufferings chiefly through the thought of his sister's possible disillusionment.

IV

WITHIN three months two events had set the studio building talking. Stanwell had painted a full-length portrait of Mrs. Archer Millington, and Caspar Arran had received an order to execute his group in marble.

The name of the sculptor's patron had not been divulged. The order came through Shepson, who explained that an American customer living abroad, having seen a photograph of the group in one of the papers, had at once cabled home to secure it. He intended to bestow it on a public building in America, and not wishing to advertise his munificence, had preferred that even the sculptor should remain ignorant of his name. The group bought by an enlightened compatriot for the adornment of a civic building in his native land! There could hardly be a more complete vindication of unappreciated genius, and Caspar made the most of the argument. He was not exultant, he was sublimely magnanimous. He had always said that he could afford to await the Verdict of Posterity, and his unknown patron's act clearly shadowed forth that impressive decision. Happily it also found expression in a cheque which it would have taken more philosophy to await. The group was paid for in advance, and Kate's joy in her brother's recognition was deliciously mingled with the thrill of ordering him some new clothes, and coaxing him out to dine succulently at a neighbouring restaurant. Caspar flourished insufferably on this regime: he began to strike the attitude of the recognized Great Master, who gives advice and encouragement to the struggling neophyte. He held himself up as an example of the reward of disinterestedness, of the triumph of the artist who clings obstinately to his convictions.

"A man must believe in his star—look at Napoleon! It's the dogged trust in one's convictions that tells—it always ends by forcing the public into line. Only be sure you make no concessions—don't give in to any of their humbug! An artist who listens to the critics is ruined—they never have any use for the poor devils who do what they tell them to. Run after fame and she'll keep you running, but stay in your own corner and do your own work, and by George, sir, she'll come crawling up to you and ask to have her likeness done!"

These exhortations were chiefly directed to Stanwell, partly because the inmates of the other studios were apt to elude them, partly also because the rumours concerning Stanwell's portrait of Mrs. Millington had begun to disquiet the sculptor. At first he had taken a condescending interest in the fact of his friend's receiving an order, and had admonished him not to lose the chance of "showing up" his sitter and her environment. It was a splendid opportunity for a fellow with a "message" to be introduced into the tents of the Philistine, and Stanwell was charged to drive a long sharp nail into the enemy's skull. But presently Arran began to suspect that the portrait was not as comminatory as he could have wished. Mungold, the most kindly of rivals, let drop a word of injudicious praise: the picture, he said, promised to be delightfully "in keeping" with the decorations of the ball-room, and the lady's gown harmonized exquisitely with the window-curtains. Stanwell, called to account by his monitor, reminded the latter that he himself had been selected by Mungold to do the Cupids for Mrs. Millington's ball-room, and that the friendly artist's praise could, therefore, not be taken as positive evidence of incapacity.

"Ah, but I didn't do them—I kicked him out!" Caspar rejoined; and Stanwell could only plead that, even in the cause of art, one could hardly kick a lady.

"Ah, that's the worst of it. If the women get at you you're lost. You're young, you're impressionable, you won't mind my saying that you're not built for a stoic, and hang it, they'll coddle you, they'll enervate you, they'll sentimentalize you, they'll make a Mungold of you!"

"Ah, poor Mungold," Stanwell laughed. "If he lived the life of an anchorite he couldn't help painting pictures that would please Mrs. Millington."

"Whereas you could," Kate interjected, raising her head from the ironing-board where, Sphinx-like, magnificent, she swung a splendid arm above her brother's shirts.

"Oh, well, perhaps I shan't please her; perhaps I shall elevate her taste."

Caspar directed a groan to his sister. "That's what they all think at first—Childe Roland to the Dark Tower came. But inside the Dark Tower there's the Venusberg. Oh, I don't mean that you'll be taken with truffles and plush footmen, like Mungold. But praise, my poor Ned—praise is a deadly drug! It's the absinthe of the artist—and they'll stupefy you with it. You'll wallow in the mire of success."

Stanwell raised a protesting hand. "Really, for one order, you're a little lurid!"

"One? Haven't you already had a dozen others?"

"Only one other, so far—and I'm not sure I shall do that."

"Not sure—wavering already! That's the way the mischief begins. If the women get a fad for you they'll work you like a galley-slave. You'll have to do your round of 'copy' every morning. What becomes of inspiration then? How are you going to loaf and invite the soul? Don't barter your birthright for a mess of pottage! Oh, I understand the temptation—I know the taste of money and success. But look at me, Stanwell. You know how long I had to wait for recognition. Well, now it's come to me I don't mean to let it knock me off my feet. I don't mean to let myself be overworked; I have already made it known that I will not be bullied into taking more orders than I can do full justice to. And my sister is with me, God bless her; Kate would rather go on ironing my shirts in a garret than see me prostitute my art!"

Kate's glance radiantly confirmed this declaration of independence, and Stanwell, with his evasive laugh, asked her if, meanwhile, she should object to his investing a part of his ill-gotten gains in theatre tickets for the party that evening.

It appeared that Stanwell had also been paid in advance, and well paid; for he began to permit himself various mild distractions, in which he generally contrived to have the Arrans share. It seemed perfectly natural to Kate that Caspar's friends should spend their money for his recreation, and by one of the most touching sophistries of her sex she thus reconciled herself to the anomaly of taking a little pleasure on her own account. Mungold was less often in the way, for she had never been able to forgive him for proposing that Caspar should do Mrs. Millington's Cupids; and for a few radiant weeks Stanwell had the undisputed enjoyment of her pride in her brother's achievement.

Stanwell had "rushed through" Mrs. Millington's portrait in time for the opening of her new ball-room; and it was perhaps in return for this favour that she consented to let the picture be exhibited at a big Portrait Show which was held in April for the benefit of a fashionable charity.

In Mrs. Millington's ball-room the picture had been seen and approved only by the distinguished few who had access to that social sanctuary; but on the walls of the exhibition it became a centre of comment and discussion. One of the immediate results of this publicity was a visit from Shepson, with two or three orders in his pocket, as he put it. He surveyed the studio with fresh disgust, asked Stanwell why he did not move, and was impressed rather than downcast on learning that the painter had not decided whether he would take any more orders that spring.

"You might haf a studio at Newport," he suggested. "It would be rather new to do your sitters out of doors, with the sea behind them—showing they had a blace on the gliffs!"

The picture produced a different and less flattering effect on the critics. They gave it, indeed, more space than they had ever before accorded to the artist's efforts, but their estimate seemed to confirm Caspar Arran's forebodings, and Stanwell had perhaps never despised them so little as when he read their comments on his work. On the whole, however, neither praise nor blame disquieted him greatly. He was engrossed in the contemplation of Kate Arran's happiness, and basking in the refracted warmth it shed about her. The doctor's prognostications had come true. Caspar was putting on a pound a week, and had plunged into a fresh "creation" more symbolic and encumbering than the monument of which he had been so opportunely relieved. If there was any cloud on Stanwell's enjoyment of life, it was caused by the discovery that success had quadrupled Caspar's artistic energies. Meanwhile it was delightful to see Kate's joy in her brother's recovered capacity for work, and to listen to the axioms which, for Stanwell's guidance, she deduced from the example of Caspar's heroic pursuit of the ideal. There was nothing repellent in Kate's borrowed didacticism, and if it sometimes bored Stanwell to hear her quote her brother, he was sure it would never bore him to be quoted by her himself; and there were moments when he felt he had nearly achieved that distinction.

Caspar was not addicted to the visiting of art exhibitions. He took little interest in any productions save his own, and was moreover disposed to believe that good pictures, like clever criminals, are apt to go unhung. Stanwell therefore thought it unlikely that his portrait of Mrs. Millington would be seen by Kate, who was not given to independent explorations in the field of art; but one day, on entering the exhibition—which he had hitherto rather nervously shunned—he saw the Arrans at the end of the gallery in which the portrait hung. They were not looking at it, they were moving away from it, and to Stanwell's quickened perceptions their attitude seemed almost that of flight. For a moment he thought of flying too; then a desperate resolve nerved him to meet them, and stemming the crowd, he made a circuit which brought him face to face with their retreat.

The room in which they met was momentarily empty, and there was nothing to intervene between the shock of their inter-changed glances. Caspar was flushed and bristling: his little body quivered like a machine from which the steam has just been turned off. Kate lifted a stricken glance. Stanwell read in it the reflexion of her brother's tirade, but she held out her hand in silence.

For a moment Caspar was silent too; then, with a terrible smile: "My dear fellow, I congratulate you; Mungold will have to look to his laurels," he said.

The shot delivered, he stalked away with his seven-league stride, and Kate moved tragically through the room in his wake.

V

SHEPSON took up his hat with a despairing gesture.

"Vell, I gif you up—I gif you up!" he said.

"Don't—yet," protested Stanwell from the divan.

It was winter again, and though the janitor had not forgotten the fire, the studio gave no other evidence of its master's increasing prosperity. If Stanwell spent his money it was not upon himself.

He leaned back against the wall, his hands in his pockets, a cigarette between his lips, while Shepson paced the dirty floor or halted impatiently before an untouched canvas on the easel.

"I tell you vat it is, Mr. Sdanwell, I can't make you out!" he lamented. "Last vinter you got a sdart that vould have kept most men going for years. After making dat hit vith Mrs. Millington's picture you could have bainted half the town. And here you are sitting on your divan and saying you can't make up your mind to take another order. Vell, I can only say that if you take much longer to make it up, you'll find some other chap has cut in and got your job. Mrs. Van Orley has been waiting since last August, and she dells me you haven't even answered her letter."

"How could I? I didn't know if I wanted to paint her."

"My goodness! Don't you know if you vant three thousand tollars?"

Stanwell surveyed his cigarette. "No, I'm not sure I do," he said.

Shepson flung out his hands. "Ask more den—but do it quick!" he exclaimed.

Left to himself, Stanwell stood in silent contemplation of the canvas on which the dealer had riveted his reproachful gaze. It had been destined to reflect the opulent image of Mrs. Alpheus Van Orley, but some secret reluctance of Stanwell's had stayed the execution of the task. He had painted two of Mrs. Millington's friends in the spring, had been much praised and liberally paid for his work, and then, declining several recent orders to be executed at Newport, had surprised his friends by remaining quietly in town. It was not till August that he hired a little cottage on the New Jersey coast and invited the Arrans to visit him. They accepted the invitation, and the three had spent together six weeks of seashore idleness, during which Stanwell's modest rafters shook with Caspar's denunciations of his host's venality, and the brightness of Kate's gratitude was tempered by a tinge of reproach. But her grief over Stanwell's apostasy could not efface the fact that he had offered her brother the means of escape from town, and Stanwell himself was consoled by the reflection that but for Mrs. Millington's portrait he could not have performed even this trifling service for his friends.

When the Arrans left him in September he went to pay a few visits in the country, and on his return, a month later, to the studio building he found things had not gone well with Caspar. The little sculptor had caught cold, and the labour and expense of converting his gigantic off-spring into marble seemed to hang heavily upon him. He and Kate were living in a damp company of amorphous clay monsters, unfinished witnesses to the creative frenzy which had seized him after the sale of his group; and the doctor had urged that his patient should be removed to warmer and drier lodgings. But to uproot Caspar was impossible, and his sister could only feed the stove, and swaddle him in mufflers and felt slippers.

Stanwell found that during his absence Mungold had reappeared, fresh and rosy from a summer in Europe, and as prodigal as ever of the only form of attention which Kate could be counted on not to resent. The game and champagne reappeared with him, and he seemed as ready as Stanwell to lend a patient ear to Caspar's homilies. But Stanwell could see that, even now, Kate had not forgiven him for the Cupids. Stanwell himself had spent the early winter months in idleness. The sight of his tools filled him with a strange repugnance, and he absented himself as much as possible from the studio. But Shepson's visit roused him to the fact that he must decide on some definite course of action. If he wished to follow up his success of the previous spring he must refuse no more orders: he must not let Mrs. Van Orley slip away from him. He knew there were competitors enough ready to profit by his hesitations, and since his success was the result of a whim, a whim might undo it. With a sudden gesture of decision he caught up his hat and left the studio.

On the landing he met Kate Arran. She too was going out, drawn forth by the sudden radiance of the January afternoon. She met him with a smile which seemed the answer to his uncertainties, and he asked abruptly if she had time to take a walk with him.

Yes; for once she had time, for Mr. Mungold was sitting with Caspar, and had promised to remain till she came in. It mattered little to Stanwell that Mungold was with Caspar as long as he himself was with Kate; and he instantly soared to the suggestion that they should prolong the painter's vigil by taking the "elevated" to the Park. In this too his companion acquiesced after a moment of surprise: she seemed in a consenting mood, and Stanwell augured well from the fact.

The Park was clothed in the double glitter of snow and sunshine. They roamed the hard white alleys to a continuous tinkle of sleigh-bells, and Kate brightened with the exhilaration of the scene. It was not often that she permitted herself such an escape from routine, and in this new environment, which seemed to detach her from her daily setting, Stanwell had his first complete vision of her. To the girl also their unwonted isolation seemed to create a sense of fuller communion, for she began presently, as they reached the leafless solitude of the Ramble, to speak with sudden freedom of her brother. It appeared that the orders against which Caspar had so heroically steeled himself were slow in coming: he had received no commission since the sale of his group, and he was beginning to suffer from a reaction of discouragement. Oh, it was not the craving for popularity—Stanwell knew how far above that he stood. But it had been exquisite, yes, exquisite to him to find himself believed in, understood. He had fancied that the purchase of the group was the dawn of a tardy recognition—and now the darkness of indifference had set in again, no one spoke of him, no one wrote of him, no one cared.

"If he were in good health it would not matter—he would throw off such weakness, he would live only for the joy of his work; but he is losing ground, his strength is failing, and he is so afraid there will not be time enough left—time enough for full recognition," she explained.

The quiver in her voice silenced Stanwell: he was afraid of echoing it with his own. At length he said: "Oh, more orders will come. Success is a gradual growth."

"Yes, *real* success," she said, with a solemn note in which he caught—and forgave—a reflection on his own facile triumphs.

"But when the orders do come," she continued, "will he have strength to carry them out? Last winter the doctor thought he only needed work to set him up; now he talks of rest instead! He says we ought to go to a warm climate—but how can Caspar leave the group?"

"Oh, hang the group—let him chuck the order!" cried Stanwell.

She looked at him tragically. "The money is spent," she said.

He coloured to the roots of his hair. "But ill-health—ill-health excuses everything. If he goes away now he will come back good for twice the amount of work in the spring. A sculptor is not expected to deliver a statue on a given day, like a package of groceries! You must do as the doctor says—you must make him chuck everything and go."

They had reached a windless nook above the lake, and, pausing in the stress of their talk, she let herself sink on a bench beside the path. The movement encouraged him, and he seated himself at her side.

"You must take him away at once," he repeated urgently. "He must be made comfortable—you must both be free from worry. And I want you to let me manage it for you—"

He broke off, silenced by her rising blush, her protesting murmur.

"Oh, stop, please; let me explain. I'm not talking of lending you money; I'm talking of giving you—myself. The offer may be just as unacceptable, but it's of a kind to which it's customary to accord it a hearing. I should have made it a year ago—the first day I saw you, I believe!—but that, then, it wasn't in my power to make things easier for you. But now, you know, I've had a little luck. Since I painted Mrs. Millington things have changed. I believe I can get as many orders as I choose—there are two or three people waiting now. What's the use of it all, if it doesn't bring me a little happiness? And the only happiness I know is the kind that you can give me."

He paused, suddenly losing the courage to look at her, so that her pained murmur was framed for him in a glittering vision of the frozen lake. He turned with a start and met the refusal in her eyes.

"No—really no?" he repeated.

She shook her head silently.

"I could have helped you—I could have helped you!" he sighed.

She flushed distressfully, but kept her eyes on his.

"It's just that—don't you see?" she reproached him.

"Just that—the fact that I could be of use to you?"

"The fact that, as you say, things have changed since you painted Mrs. Millington. I haven't seen the later portraits, but they tell me—"

"Oh, they're just as bad!" Stanwell jeered.

"You've sold your talent, and you know it: that's the dreadful part. You did it deliberately," she cried with passion.

"Oh, deliberately," he interjected.

"And you're not ashamed—you talk of going on."

"I'm not ashamed; I talk of going on."

She received this with a long shuddering sigh, and turned her eyes away from him.

"Oh, why—why—why?" she lamented.

It was on the tip of Stanwell's tongue to answer, "That I might say to you what I am just saying now—" but he replied instead: "A man may paint bad pictures and be a decent fellow. Look at Mungold, after all!"

The adjuration had an unexpected effect. Kate's colour faded suddenly, and she sat motionless, with a stricken face.

"There's a difference—" she began at length abruptly; "the difference you've always insisted on. Mr. Mungold paints as well as he can. He has no idea that his pictures are—less good than they might be."

"Well—?"

"So he can't be accused of doing what he does for money—of sacrificing anything better." She turned on him with troubled eyes. "It was you who made me understand that, when Caspar used to make fun of him."

Stanwell smiled. "I'm glad you still think me a better painter than Mungold. But isn't it hard that for that very reason I should starve in a hole? If I painted badly enough you'd see no objection to my living at the Waldorf!"

"Ah, don't joke about it," she murmured. "Don't triumph in it."

"I see no reason to at present," said Stanwell drily. "But I won't pretend to be ashamed when I'm not. I think there are occasions when a man is justified in doing what I've done."

She looked at him solemnly. "What occasions?"

"Why, when he wants money, hang it!"

She drew a deep breath. "Money—money? Has Caspar's example been nothing to you, then?"

"It hasn't proved to me that I must starve while Mungold lives on truffles!"

Again her face changed and she stirred uneasily, and then rose to her feet.

"There is no occasion which can justify an artist's sacrificing his convictions!" she exclaimed.

Stanwell rose too, facing her with a mounting urgency which sent a flush to his cheek.

"Can't you conceive such an occasion in my case? The wish, I mean, to make things easier for Caspar—to help you in any way you might let me?"

Her face reflected his blush, and she stood gazing at him with a wounded wonder.

"Caspar and I—you imagine we could live on money earned in *that* way?"

Stanwell made an impatient gesture. "You've got to live on something—or he has, even if you don't include yourself!"

Her blush deepened miserably, but she held her head high.

"That's just it—that's what I came here to say to you." She stood a moment gazing away from him at the lake.

He looked at her in surprise. "You came here to say something to me?"

"Yes. That we've got to live on something, Caspar and I, as you say; and since an artist cannot sacrifice his convictions, the sacrifice must—I mean—I wanted you to know that I have promised to marry Mr. Mungold."

"Mungold!" Stanwell cried with a sharp note of irony; but her white look checked it on his lips.

"I know all you are going to say," she murmured, with a kind of nobleness which moved him even through his sense of its grotesqueness. "But you must see the distinction, because you first made it clear to me. I can take money earned in good faith—I can let Caspar live on it. I can marry Mr. Mungold; because, though his pictures are bad, he does not prostitute his art."

She began to move away from him slowly, and he followed her in silence along the frozen path.

When Stanwell re-entered his studio the dusk had fallen. He lit his lamp and rummaged out some writing-materials. Having found them, he wrote to Shepson to say that he could not paint Mrs. Van Orley, and did not care to accept any more orders for the present. He sealed and stamped the letter and flung it over the banisters for the janitor to post; then he dragged out his unfinished head of Kate Arran, replaced it on the easel, and sat down before it with a grim smile.

THE BEST MAN

I

Dusk had fallen, and the circle of light shed by the lamp of Governor Mornway's writing-table just rescued from the surrounding dimness his own imposing bulk, thrown back in a deep chair in the lounging attitude habitual to him at that hour.

When the Governor of Midsylvania rested he rested completely. Five minutes earlier he had been bowed over his office desk, an Atlas with the State on his shoulders; now, his working hours over, he had the air of a man who has spent his day in desultory pleasure, and means to end it in the enjoyment of a good dinner. This freedom from care threw into relief the hovering fidgetiness of his sister, Mrs. Nimick, who, just outside the circle of lamplight, haunted the warm gloom of the hearth, from which the wood fire now and then sent up an exploring flash into her face.

Mrs. Nimick's presence did not usually minister to repose; but the Governor's serenity was too deep to be easily disturbed, and he felt the calmness of a man who knows there is a mosquito in the room, but has drawn the netting close about his head. This calmness reflected itself in the accent with which he said, throwing himself back to smile up at his sister: "You know I am not going to make any appointments for a week."

It was the day after the great reform victory which had put John Mornway for the second time at the head of his State, a triumph compared with which even the mighty battle of his first election sank into insignificance, and he leaned back with the sense of unassailable placidity which follows upon successful effort.

Mrs. Nimick murmured an apology. "I didn't understand—I saw in this morning's papers that the Attorney-General was reappointed."

"Oh, Fleetwood—his reappointment was involved in the campaign. He's one of the principles I represent!"

Mrs. Nimick smiled a little tartly. "It seems odd to some people to think of Mr. Fleetwood in connection with principles."

The Governor's smile had no answering acerbity; the mention of his Attorney-General's name had set his blood humming with the thrill of the fight, and he wondered how it was that Fleetwood had not already been in to clasp hands with him over their triumph.

"No," he said, good-humoredly, "two years ago Fleetwood's name didn't stand for principles of any sort; but I believed in him, and look what he's done for me! I thought he was too big a man not to see in time that statesmanship is a finer thing than practical politics, and now that I've given him a chance to make the discovery, he's on the way to becoming just such a statesman as the country needs."

"Oh, it's a great deal easier and pleasanter to believe in people," replied Mrs. Nimick, in a tone full of occult allusion, "and, of course, we all knew that Mr. Fleetwood would have a hearing before any one else."

The Governor took this imperturbably. "Well, at any rate, he isn't going to fill all the offices in the State; there will probably be one or two to spare after he has helped himself, and when the time comes I'll think over your man. I'll consider him."

Mrs. Nimick brightened. "It would make *such* a difference to Jack—it might mean anything to the poor boy to have Mr. Ashford appointed!"

The Governor held up a warning hand.

"Oh, I know, one mustn't say that, or at least you mustn't listen. You're so dreadfully afraid of nepotism. But I'm not asking for anything for Jack—I have never asked for a crust for any of us, thank Heaven! No one can point to *me*—" Mrs. Nimick checked herself suddenly and continued in a more impersonal tone: "But there's no harm, surely, in my saying a word for Mr. Ashford, when I know that he's actually under consideration, and I don't see why the fact that Jack is in his office should prevent my speaking."

"On the contrary," said the Governor, "it implies, on your part, a personal knowledge of Mr. Ashford's qualifications which may be of great help to me in reaching a decision."

Mrs. Nimick never quite knew how to meet him when he took that tone, and the flickering fire made her face for a moment the picture of uncertainty; then at all hazards she launched out: "Well, I have Ella's promise, at any rate."

The Governor sat upright. "Ella's promise?"

"To back me up. She thoroughly approves of him!"

The Governor smiled. "You talk as if Ella had a political *salon* and distributed *lettres de cachet!* I'm glad she approves of Ashford; but if you think my wife makes my appointments for me—" He broke off with a laugh at the superfluity of such a protest.

Mrs. Nimick reddened. "One never knows how you will take the simplest thing. What harm is there in my saying that Ella approves of Mr. Ashford? I thought you liked her to take an interest in your work."

"I like it immensely. But I shouldn't care to have it take that form."

"What form?"

"That of promising to use her influence to get people appointed. But you always talk of politics in the vocabulary of European courts. Thank Heaven, Ella has less imagination. She has her sympathies, of course, but she doesn't think they can affect the distribution of offices."

Mrs. Nimick gathered up her furs with an air at once crestfallen and resentful. "I'm sorry—I always seem to say the wrong thing. I'm sure I came with the best intentions—it's natural that your sister should want to be with you at such a happy moment."

"Of course it is, my dear," exclaimed the Governor genially, as he rose to grasp the hands with which she was nervously adjusting her wraps.

Mrs. Nimick, who lived a little way out of town, and whose visits to her brother were apparently achieved at the cost of immense effort and mysterious complications, had come to congratulate him on his victory, and to sound him regarding the nomination to a coveted post of the lawyer in whose firm her eldest son was a clerk. In the urgency of the latter errand she had rather lost sight of the former, but her face softened as the Governor, keeping both her hands in his, said in the voice which always seemed to put the most generous interpretation on her motives: "I was sure you would be one of the first to give me your blessing."

"Oh, your success—no one feels it more than I do!" sighed Mrs. Nimick, always at home in the emotional key. "I keep in the background. I make no noise, I claim no credit, but whatever happens, no one shall ever prevent my rejoicing in my brother's success!"

Mrs. Nimick's felicitations were always couched in the conditional, with a side-glance at dark contingencies, and the Governor, smiling at the familiar construction, returned cheerfully: "I don't see why any one should want to deprive you of that privilege."

"They couldn't—they couldn't—" Mrs. Nimick heroically affirmed.

"Well, I'm in the saddle for another two years at any rate, so you had better put in all the rejoicing you can."

"Whatever happens—whatever happens!" cried Mrs. Nimick, melting on his bosom.

"The only thing likely to happen at present is that you will miss your train if I let you go on saying nice things to me much longer."

Mrs. Nimick at this dried her eyes, renewed her clutch on her draperies, and stood glancing sentimentally about the room while her brother rang for the carriage.

"I take away a lovely picture of you," she murmured. "It's wonderful what you've made of this hideous house."

"Ah, not I, but Ella—there she *does* reign undisputed," he acknowledged, following her glance about the library, which wore an air of permanent habitation, of slowly formed intimacy with its inmates, in marked contrast to the gaudy impersonality of the usual executive apartment.

"Oh, she's wonderful, quite wonderful. I see she has got those imported damask curtains she was looking at the other day at Fielding's. When I am asked how she does it all, I always say it's beyond me!" Mrs. Nimick murmured.

"It's an art like another," smiled the Governor. "Ella has been used to living in tents and she has the knack of giving them a wonderful look of permanence."

"She certainly makes the most extraordinary bargains—all the knack in the world won't take the place of such curtains and carpets."

"Are they good? I'm glad to hear it. But all the good curtains and carpets won't make a house comfortable to live in. There's where the knack comes in, you see."

He recalled with a shudder the lean Congressional years—the years before his marriage—when Mrs. Nimick had lived with him in Washington, and the daily struggle in the House had been combined with domestic conflicts almost equally recurrent. The offer of a foreign mission, though disconnecting him from active politics, had the advantage of freeing him from his sister's tutelage, and in Europe, where he remained for two years, he had met the lady who was to become his wife. Mrs. Renfield was the widow of one of the diplomatists who languish in perpetual first secretary-ship at our various embassies. Her life had given her ease without triviality, and a sense of the importance of politics seldom found in ladies of her nationality. She regarded a public life as the noblest and most engrossing of careers, and combined with great social versatility an equal gift for reading blue-books and studying debates. So sincere was the latter taste that she passed without regret from the amenities of a European life well stocked with picturesque intimacies to the rawness of the Midsylvanian capital. She helped Mornway in his fight for the Governorship as a man likes to be helped by a woman—by her tact, her good looks, her memory for faces, her knack of saying the right thing to the right person, and her capacity for obscure hard work in the background of his public activity. But, above all, she helped him by making his private life smooth and harmonious. For a man careless of personal ease, Mornway was singularly alive to the domestic amenities. Attentive service, well-ordered dinners, brightly burning fires, and a scent of flowers in the house—these material details, which had come to seem the extension of his wife's personality, the inevitable result of her nearness, were as agreeable to him after five years of marriage as in the first surprise of his introduction to them. Mrs. Nimick had kept house jerkily and vociferously; Ella performed the same task silently and imperceptibly, and the results were all in favor of the latter method. Though neither the Governor nor his wife had large means, the household, under Mrs. Mornway's guidance, took on an air of sober luxury as agreeable to her husband as it was exasperating to her sister-in-law. The domestic machinery ran without a jar. There were no upheavals, no debts, no squalid cookless hiatuses between intervals of showy hospitality; the household moved along on lines of quiet elegance and comfort, behind which only the eye of the housekeeping sex could have detected a gradually increasing scale of expense.

Such an eye was now projected on the Governor's surroundings, and its explorations were summed up in the tone in which Mrs. Nimick repeated from the threshold: "I always say I don't see how she does it!"

The tone did not escape the Governor, but it disturbed him no more than the buzz of a baffled insect. Poor Grace! It was not his fault if her husband was given to chimerical investments, if her sons were "unsatisfactory," and her cooks would not stay with her; but it was natural that these facts should throw into irritating contrast the ease and harmony of his own domestic life. It made him all the sorrier for his sister to know that her envy did not penetrate to the essence of his happiness, but lingered on those external signs of well-being which counted for so little in the sum total of his advantages. Poor Mrs. Nimick's life seemed doubly thin and mean when one remembered that, beneath its shabby surface, there were no compensating riches of the spirit.

II

IT was the custodian of his own hidden treasure who at this moment broke in upon his musings. Mrs. Mornway, fresh from her afternoon walk, entered the room with that air of ease and lightness which seemed to diffuse a social warmth about her; fine, slender, pliant, so polished and modeled by an intelligent experience of life that youth seemed clumsy in her presence. She looked down at her husband and shook her head.

"You promised to keep the afternoon to yourself, and I hear Grace has been here."

"Poor Grace—she didn't stay long, and I should have been a brute not to see her."

He leaned back, filling his gaze to the brim with her charming image, which obliterated at a stroke the fretful ghost of Mrs. Nimick.

"She came to congratulate you, I suppose?"

"Yes, and to ask me to do something for Ashford."

"Ah—on account of Jack. What does she want for him?"

The Governor laughed. "She said you were in her confidence—that you were backing her up. She seemed to think your support would ensure her success."

Mrs. Mornway smiled; her smile, always full of delicate implications, seemed to caress her husband while it gently mocked his sister.

"Poor Grace! I suppose you undeceived her."

"As to your influence? I told her it was paramount where it ought to be."

"And where is that?"

"In the choice of carpets and curtains. It seems ours are almost too good."

"Thanks for the compliment! Too good for what?"

"Our station in life, I suppose. At least they seemed to bother Grace."

"Poor Grace! I've always bothered her." She paused, removing her gloves reflectively and laying her long fine hands on his shoulders as she stood behind him. "Then you don't believe in Ashford?" Feeling his slight start, she drew away her hands and raised them to detach her veil.

"What makes you think I don't believe in Ashford?" he asked.

"I asked out of curiosity. I wondered whether you had decided anything."

"No, and I don't mean to for a week. I'm dead beat, and I want to bring a fresh mind to the question. There is hardly one appointment I'm sure of except, of course, Fleetwood's."

She turned away from him, smoothing her hair in the mirror above the mantelpiece. "You're sure of that?" she asked after a moment.

"Of George Fleetwood? And poor Grace thinks you are deep in my counsels! I am as sure of re-appointing Fleetwood as I am that I have just been re-elected myself. I've never made any secret of the fact that if they wanted me back they must have him, too."

"You are tremendously generous!" she murmured.

"Generous? What a strange word to use! Fleetwood is my trump card—the one man I can count on to carry out my ideas through thick and thin."

She mused on this, smiling a little. "That's why I call you generous—when I remember how you disliked him two years ago!"

"What of that? I was prejudiced against him, I own; or rather, I had a just distrust of a man with such a past. But how splendidly he's wiped it out! What a record he has written on the new leaf he promised to turn over if I gave him the chance! Do you know," the Governor interrupted himself with a pleasantly reminiscent laugh, "I was rather annoyed with Grace when she hinted that you had promised to back up Ashford—I told her you didn't aspire to distribute patronage. But she might have reminded me—if she'd known—that it *was* you who persuaded me to give Fleetwood that chance."

Mrs. Mornway turned with a slight heightening of color. "Grace—how could she possibly have known?"

"She couldn't, of course, unless she'd read my weakness in my face. But why do you look so startled at my little joke?"

"It's only that I so dislike Grace's ineradicable idea that I am a wire-puller. Why should she imagine I would help her about Ashford?"

"Oh, Grace has always been a mild and ineffectual conspirator, and she thinks every other woman is built on the same plan. But you *did* get Fleetwood's job for him, you know," he repeated with laughing insistence.

"I had more faith than you in human nature, that's all." She paused a moment, and then added: "Personally, you know, I have always rather disliked him."

"Oh, I never doubted your disinterestedness. But you are not going to turn against your candidate, are you?"

She hesitated. "I am not sure; circumstances alter cases. When you made Fleetwood Attorney-General two years ago he was the inevitable man for the place."

"Well—is there a better one now?"

"I don't say there is—it's not my business to look for him, at any rate. What I mean is that at that time Fleetwood was worth risking anything for—now I don't know that he is."

"But, even if he were not, what do I risk for him now? I don't see your point. Since he didn't cost me my re-election, what can he possibly cost me now I'm in?"

"He's immensely unpopular. He will cost you a great deal of popularity, and you have never pretended to despise that."

"No, nor ever sacrificed anything essential to it. Are you really asking me to offer up Fleetwood to it now?"

"I don't ask you to do anything—except to consider if he *is* essential. You said you were over-tired and wanted to bring a fresh mind to bear on the other appointments. Why not delay this one too?"

Mornway turned in his chair and looked at her searchingly. "This means something, Ella. What have you heard?"

"Just what you have, probably, but with more attentive ears. The very record you are so proud of has made George Fleetwood innumerable enemies in the last two years. The Lead Trust people are determined to ruin him, and if his reappointment is attacked you will not be spared."

"Attacked? In the papers, you mean?"

She paused. "You know the 'Spy' has always threatened a campaign. And he has a past, as you say."

"Which was public property long before I first appointed him. Nothing could be gained by raking up his old political history. Everybody knows he didn't come to me with clean hands, but to hurt him now the 'Spy' would have to fasten a new scandal on him, and that would not be easy."

"It would be easy to invent one!"

"Unproved accusations don't count much against a man of such proved capacity. The best answer is his record of the last two years. That is what the public looks at."

"The public looks wherever the press points. And besides, you have your own future to consider. It would be a pity to sacrifice such a career as yours for the sake of backing up even as useful a man as George Fleetwood." She paused, as if checked by his gathering frown, but went on with fresh decision: "Oh, I'm not speaking of personal ambition; I'm thinking of the good you can do. Will Fleetwood's reappointment secure the greatest good of the greatest number, if his unpopularity reacts on you to the extent of hindering your career?"

The Governor's brow cleared and he rose with a smile. "My dear, your reasoning is admirable, but we must leave my career to take care of itself. Whatever I may be to-morrow, I am Governor of Midsylvania to-day, and my business as Governor is to appoint as Attorney-General the best man I can find for the place—and that man is George Fleetwood, unless you have a better one to propose." She met this with perfect good-humor. "No, I have told you already that that is not my business. But I *have* a candidate of my own for another office, so Grace was not quite wrong, after all."

"Well, who is your candidate, and for what office? I only hope you don't want to change cooks!"

"Oh, I do that without your authority, and you never even know it has been done." She hesitated, and then said with a bright directness: "I want you to do something for poor Gregg."

"Gregg? Rufus Gregg?" He stared. "What an extraordinary request! What can I do for a man I've had to kick out for dishonesty?"

"Not much, perhaps; I know it's difficult. But, after all, it was your kicking him out that ruined him."

"It was his dishonesty that ruined him. He was getting a good salary as my stenographer, and if he hadn't sold those letters to the 'Spy' he would have been getting it still."

She wavered. "After all, nothing was proved—he always denied it."

"Good heavens, Ella! Have you ever doubted his guilt?"

"No—no; I don't mean that. But, of course, his wife and children believe in him, and think you were cruel, and he has been out of work so long that they are starving."

"Send them some money, then; I wonder you thought it necessary to ask."

"I shouldn't have thought it so, but money is not what I want. Mrs. Gregg is proud, and it is hard to help her in that way. Couldn't you give him work of some kind—just a little post in a corner?"

"My dear child, the little posts in the corner are just the ones where honesty is essential. A footpad doesn't wait under a street-lamp! Besides, how can I recommend a man whom I have dismissed for theft? I won't say a word to hinder his getting a place, but on my conscience I can't give him one."

She paused and turned toward the door silently, though without any show of resentment; but on the threshold she lingered long enough to say: "Yet you gave Fleetwood his chance!"

"Fleetwood? You class Fleetwood with Gregg? The best man in the State with a little beggarly thieving nonentity? It's evident enough you're new at wire-pulling, or you would show more skill at it!"

She met this with a laugh. "I'm not likely to have much practice if my first attempt is such a failure. Well, I will see if Mrs. Gregg will let me help her a little—I suppose there is nothing else to be done."

"Nothing that we can do. If Gregg wants a place he had better get one on the staff of the 'Spy.' He served them better than he did me."

III

THE Governor stared at the card with a frown. Half an hour had elapsed since his wife had gone upstairs to dress for the big dinner from which official duties excused him, and he was still lingering over the fire before preparing for his own solitary meal. He expected no one that evening but his old friend Hadley Shackwell, with whom it was his long-established habit to talk over his defeats and victories in the first lull after the conflict; and Shackwell was not likely to turn up till nine o'clock. The unwonted stillness of the room, and the knowledge that he had a quiet evening before him, filled the Governor with a luxurious sense of repose. The world seemed to him a good place to be in, and his complacency was shadowed only by the fear that he had perhaps been a trifle over-harsh in refusing his wife's plea for the stenographer. There seemed, therefore, a certain fitness in the appearance of the man's card, and the Governor with a sigh gave orders that Gregg should be shown in.

Gregg was still the soft-stepping scoundrel who invited the toe of honesty, and Mornway, as he entered, was conscious of a sharp revulsion of feeling. But it was impossible to evade the interview, and he sat silent while the man stated his case.

Mrs. Mornway had represented the stenographer as being in desperate straits, and ready to accept any job that could be found, but though his appearance might have seemed to corroborate her account, he evidently took a less hopeless view of his case, and the Governor found with surprise that he had fixed his eye on a clerkship in one of the Government offices, a post which had been half promised him before the incident of the letters. His plea was that the Governor's charge, though unproved, had so injured his reputation that he could only hope to clear himself by getting some sort of small job under the

Administration. After that, it would be easy for him to obtain any employment he wanted.

He met Mornway's refusal with civility, but remarked after a moment: "I hadn't expected this, Governor. Mrs. Mornway led me to think that something might be arranged."

The Governor's tone was brief. "Mrs. Mornway is sorry for your wife and children, and for their sake would be glad to find work for you, but she could not have led you to think that there was any chance of your getting a clerkship."

"Well, that's just it; she said she thought she could manage it."

"You have misinterpreted my wife's interest in your family. Mrs. Mornway has nothing to do with the distribution of Government offices." The Governor broke off, annoyed to find himself asseverating for the second time so obvious a fact.

There was a moment's silence; then Gregg said, still in a perfectly equable tone: "You've always been hard on me, Governor, but I don't bear malice. You accused me of selling those letters to the 'Spy'—"

The Governor made an impatient gesture.

"You couldn't prove your case," Gregg went on imperturbably, "but you were right in one respect. I *was* on confidential terms with the 'Spy.'" He paused and glanced at Mornway, whose face remained immovable. "I'm on the same terms with them still, and I'm ready to let you have the benefit of it if you'll give *me* the chance to retrieve my good name."

In spite of his irritation the Governor could not repress a smile.

"In other words, you will do a dirty trick for me if I undertake to convince people that you are the soul of honor."

Gregg smiled also.

"There are always two ways of putting a thing. Why not call it a plain case of give and take? I want something and can pay for it."

"Not in any coin I have a use for," said Mornway, pushing back his chair.

Gregg hesitated; then he said: "Perhaps you don't mean to reappoint Fleetwood." The Governor was silent, and he continued: "If you do, don't kick me out a second time. I'm not threatening you—I'm speaking as a friend. Mrs. Mornway has been kind to my wife, and I'd like to help her."

The Governor rose, gripping his chair-back sternly. "You will be kind enough to leave my wife's name out of the discussion. I supposed you knew me well enough to know that I don't buy newspaper secrets at any price, least of all at that of the public money!"

Gregg, who had risen also, stood a few feet off, looking at him inscrutably.

"Is that final, Governor?"

"Quite final."

"Well, good evening, then."

IV

SHACKWELL and the Governor sat over the evening embers. It was after ten o'clock, and the servant had carried away the coffee and liqueurs, leaving the two men to their cigars. Mornway had once more lapsed into his arm-chair, and sat with out-stretched feet, gazing comfortably at his friend.

Shackwell was a small dry man of fifty, with a face as sallow and freckled as a winter pear, a limp mustache, and shrewd, melancholy eyes.

"I am glad you have given yourself a day's rest," he said, looking at the Governor.

"Well, I don't know that I needed it. There's such exhilaration in victory that I never felt fresher."

"Ah, but the fight's just beginning."

"I know—but I'm ready for it. You mean the campaign against Fleetwood. I understand there is to be a big row. Well, he and I are used to rows."

Shackwell paused, surveying his cigar. "You knew the 'Spy' meant to lead the attack?"

"Yes. I was offered a glimpse of the documents this afternoon."

Shackwell started up. "You didn't refuse?"

Mornway related the incident of Gregg's visit. "I could hardly buy my information at that price," he said, "and, besides, it is really Fleetwood's business this time. I suppose he has heard the report, but it doesn't seem to bother him. I rather thought he would have looked in to-day to talk things over, but I haven't seen him."

Shackwell continued to twist his cigar through his sallow fingers without remembering to light it. "You're determined to reappoint Fleetwood?" he asked at length.

The Governor caught him up. "You're the fourth person who has asked me that to-day! You haven't lost faith in him, have you, Hadley?"

"Not an atom!" said the other with emphasis.

"Well, then, what are you all thinking of, to suppose I can be frightened by a little newspaper talk? Besides, if Fleetwood is not afraid, why should I be?"

"Because you'll be involved in it with him."

The Governor laughed. "What have they got against me now?"

Shackwell, standing up, confronted his friend solemnly. "This—that Fleetwood bought his appointment two years ago."

"Ah—bought it of me? Why didn't it come out at the time?"

"Because it wasn't known then. It has only been found out lately."

"Known—found out? This is magnificent! What was my price, and what did I do with the money?"

Shackwell glanced about the room, and his eyes returned to Mornway's face.

"Look here, John, Fleetwood is not the only man in the world."

"The only man?"

"The only Attorney-General. "The 'Spy' has the Lead Trust behind it and means to put up a savage fight. Mud sticks, and—"

"Hadley, is this a conspiracy? You're saying to me just what Ella said this afternoon."

At the mention of Mrs. Mornway's name a silence fell between the two men and the Governor moved uneasily in his chair.

"You are not advising me to chuck Fleetwood because the 'Spy' is going to accuse me of having sold him his first appointment?" he said at length.

Shackwell drew a deep breath. "You say yourself that Mrs. Mornway gave you the same advice this afternoon."

"Well, what of that? Do you imagine that my wife distrib—" The Governor broke off with an exasperated laugh.

Shackwell, leaning against the mantelpiece, looked down into the embers. "I didn't say the 'Spy' meant to accuse *you* of having sold the office."

Mornway stood up slowly, his eyes on his friend's averted face. The ashes dropped from his cigar, scattering a white trail across the carpet which had excited Mrs. Nimick's envy.

"The office is in my gift. If I didn't sell it, who did?" he demanded.

Shackwell laid a hand on his arm. "For heaven's sake, John—"

"Who did, who did?" the Governor violently repeated.

The two men faced each other in the closely curtained silence of the dim luxurious room. Shackwell's eyes again wandered, as if summoning the walls to reply. Then he said, "I have positive information that the 'Spy' will say nothing if you don't appoint Fleetwood."

"And what will it say if I do appoint him?"

"That he bought his first appointment from your wife."

The Governor stood silent, immovable, while the blood crept slowly from his strong neck to his lowering brows. Once he laughed, then he set his lips and continued to gaze into the fire. After a while he looked at his cigar and shook the freshly formed cone of ashes carefully upon the hearth. He had just turned again to Shackwell when the door opened and the butler announced: "Mr. Fleetwood."

The room swam about Shackwell, and when he recovered himself, Mornway, with outstretched hand, was advancing quietly to meet his guest.

Fleetwood was a smaller man than the Governor. He was erect and compact, with a face full of dry energy, which seemed to press forward with the spring of his prominent features, as though it were the weapon with which he cleared his way through the world. He was in evening dress, scrupulously appointed, but pale and nervous. Of the two men, it was Mornway who was the more composed.

"I thought I should have seen you before this," he said.

Fleetwood returned his grasp and shook hands with Shackwell.

"I knew you needed to be let alone. I didn't mean to come to-night, but I wanted to say a word to you."

At this, Shackwell, who had fallen into the background, made a motion of leave-taking, but the Governor arrested it.

"We haven't any secrets from Hadley, have we, Fleetwood?"

"Certainly not. I am glad to have him stay. I have simply come to say that I have been thinking over my future arrangements, and that I find it will not be possible for me to continue in office."

There was a long pause, during which Shackwell kept his eyes on Mornway. The Governor had turned pale, but when he spoke his voice was full and firm.

"This is sudden," he said.

Fleetwood stood leaning against a high chair-back, fretting its carved ornaments with restless fingers. "It is sudden—yes. I—there are a variety of reasons."

"Is one of them the fact that you are afraid of what the 'Spy' is going to say?"

The Attorney-General flushed deeply and moved away a few steps. "I'm sick of mud-throwing," he muttered.

"George Fleetwood!" Mornway exclaimed. He had advanced toward his friend, and the two stood confronting each other, already oblivious of Shackwell's presence.

"It's not only that, of course. I've been frightfully hard-worked. My health has given way—"

"Since yesterday?"

Fleetwood forced a smile. "My dear fellow, what a slave-driver you are! Hasn't a man the right to take a rest?"

"Not a soldier on the eve of battle. You have never failed me before."

"I don't want to fail you now. But it isn't the eve of battle—you're in, and that's the main thing."

"The main thing at present is that you promised to stay in with me, and that I must have your real reason for breaking your word."

Fleetwood made a deprecatory movement. "My dear Governor, if you only knew it, I'm doing you a service in backing out."

"A service—why?"

"Because I'm hated—because the Lead Trust wants my blood, and will have yours too if you appoint me."

"Ah, that's the real reason, then—you're afraid of the 'Spy'?"

"Afraid—?"

The Governor continued to speak with dry deliberation. "Evidently, then, you know what they mean to say."

Fleetwood laughed. "One needn't do that to be sure it will be abominable!"

"Who cares how abominable it is if it isn't true?"

Fleetwood shrugged his shoulders and was silent. Shackwell, from a distant seat, uttered a faint protesting sound, but no one heeded him. The Governor stood squarely before Fleetwood, his hands in his pockets. "It *is* true, then?" he demanded.

"What is true?"

"What the 'Spy' means to say—that you bought my wife's influence to get your first appointment."

In the silence Shackwell started suddenly to his feet. A sound of carriage-wheels had disturbed the quiet street. They paused and then rolled up the semicircle to the door of the Executive Mansion.

"John!" Shackwell warned him.

The Governor turned impatiently; there was the sound of a servant's steps in the hall, followed by the opening and closing of the outer door.

"Your wife—Mrs. Mornway!" Shackwell cried.

Another step, accompanied by a soft rustle of skirts, was advancing toward the library.

"My wife? Let her come!" said the Governor.

V

SHE stood before them in her bright evening dress, with an arrested brilliancy of aspect like the sparkle of a fountain suddenly caught in ice. Her look moved rapidly from one to the other; then she came forward, while Shackwell slipped behind her to close the door.

"What has happened?" she said.

Shackwell began to speak, but the Governor interposed calmly:

"Fleetwood has come to tell me that he does not wish to remain in office."

"Ah!" she murmured.

There was another silence. Fleetwood broke it by saying: "It is getting late. If you want to see me to-morrow—"

The Governor looked from his face to Ella's. "Yes; go now," he said.

Shackwell moved in Fleetwood's wake to the door. Mrs. Mornway stood with her head high, smiling slightly. She shook hands with each of the men in turn; then she moved toward the sofa and laid aside her shining cloak. All her gestures were calm and noble, but as she raised her hand to unclasp the cloak her husband uttered a sudden exclamation.

"Where did you get that bracelet? I don't remember it."

"This?" She looked at him with astonishment. "It belonged to my mother. I don't often wear it."

"Ah—I shall suspect everything now," he groaned.

He turned away and flung himself with bowed head in the chair behind his writing-table. He wanted to collect himself, to question her, to get to the bottom of the hideous abyss over which his imagination hung. But what was the use? What did the facts matter? He had only to put his memories together—they led him straight to the truth. Every incident of the day seemed to point a leering finger in the same direction, from Mrs. Nimick's allusion to the imported damask curtains to Gregg's confident appeal for rehabilitation.

"If you imagine that my wife distributes patronage—" he heard himself repeating inanely, and the walls seemed to reverberate with the laughter which his sister and Gregg had suppressed. He heard Ella rise from the sofa and lifted his head sharply.

"Sit still!" he commanded. She sank back without speaking, and he hid his face again. The past months, the past years, were dancing a witches' dance about him. He remembered a hundred significant things. . . . *Oh, God,* he cried to himself, *if only she does not lie about it!* Suddenly he recalled having pitied Mrs. Nimick because she could not penetrate to the essence of his happiness. Those were the very words he had used! He heard himself laugh aloud. The clock struck—it went on striking interminably. At length he heard his wife rise again and say with sudden authority: "John, you must speak."

Authority—she spoke to him with authority! He laughed again, and through his laugh he heard the senseless rattle of the words, "If you imagine that my wife distributes patronage . . ."

He looked up haggardly and saw her standing before him. If only she would not lie about it! He said: "You see what has happened."

"I suppose some one has told you about the 'Spy.'"

"Who told you? Gregg?" he interposed.

"Yes," she said quietly.

"That was why you wanted—?"

"Why I wanted you to help him? Yes."

"Oh, God! . . . He wouldn't take money?"

"No, he wouldn't take money."

He sat silent, looking at her, noting with a morbid minuteness the exquisite finish of her dress, that finish which seemed so much a part of herself that it had never before struck him as a merely purchasable accessory. He knew so little what a woman's dresses cost! For a moment he lost himself in vague calculations; finally, he said: "What did you do it for?"

"Do what?"

"Take money from Fleetwood."

She paused a moment and then said: "If you will let me explain—"

And then he saw that, all along, he had thought she would be able to disprove it! A smothering blackness closed in on him, and he had a physical struggle for breath. Then he forced himself to his feet and said: "He was your lover?"

"Oh, no, no, *no!*" she cried with conviction. He hardly knew whether the shadow lifted or deepened; the fact that he instantly believed her seemed only to increase his bewilderment. Presently he found that she was still speaking, and he began to listen to her, catching a phrase now and then through the deafening clamor of his thoughts.

It amounted to this—that just after her husband's first election, when Fleetwood's claims for the Attorney-Generalship were being vainly pressed by a group of his political backers, Mrs. Mornway had chanced to sit next to him once or twice at dinner. One day, on the strength of these meetings, he had called and asked her frankly if she would not help him with her husband. He had made a clean breast of his past, but had said that, under a man like Mornway, he felt he could wipe out his political sins and purify himself while he served the party. She knew the party needed his brains, and she believed in him—she was sure he would keep his word. She would have spoken in his favor in any case—she would have used all her influence to overcome her husband's prejudice—and it was by a mere accident that, in the course of one of their talks, he happened to give her a "tip" (his past connections were still useful for such purposes), a "tip" which, in the first invading pressure of debt after Mornway's election, she had not had the courage to refuse. Fleetwood had made some money for her—yes, about thirty thousand dollars. She had repaid what he had lent her, and there had been no further transactions of the kind between them. But it appeared that Gregg, before his dismissal, had got hold of an old check-book which gave a hint of the story, and had pieced the rest together with the help of a clerk in Fleetwood's office. The "Spy" was in possession of the facts, but did not mean to use them if Fleetwood was not reappointed, the Lead Trust having no personal grudge against Mornway.

Her story ended there, and she sat silent while he continued to look at her. So much had perished in the wreck of his faith that he did not attach much value to what remained. It scarcely mattered that he believed her when the truth was so sordid. There had been, after all, nothing to envy him for but what Mrs. Nimick had seen; the core of his life was as mean and miserable as his sister's. . . .

His wife rose at length, pale but still calm. She had a kind of external dignity which she wore like one of her rich dresses. It seemed as little a part of her now as the finery of which his gaze contemptuously reckoned the cost.

"John—" she said, laying her hand on his shoulder.

He looked up wearily. "You had better go to bed," he interjected.

"Don't look at me in that way. I am prepared for your being angry with me—I made a dreadful mistake and must bear my punishment: any punishment you choose to inflict. But you must think of yourself first—you must spare yourself. Why should you be so horribly unhappy? Don't you see that since Mr. Fleetwood has behaved so well we are quite safe? And I swear to you I have paid back every penny of the money."

VI

THREE days later Shackwell was summoned by telephone to the Governor's office in the Capitol. There had been, in the interval, no communication between the two men, and the papers had been silent or non-committal.

In the lobby Shackwell met Fleetwood leaving the building. For a moment the Attorney-General seemed about to speak; then he nodded and passed on, leaving to Shackwell the impression of a face more than ever thrust forward like a weapon.

The Governor sat behind his desk in the clear autumn sunlight. In contrast to Fleetwood he seemed relaxed and unwieldy, and the face he turned to his friend had a gray look of convalescence. Shackwell wondered, with a start of apprehension, if he and Fleetwood had been together.

He relieved himself of his overcoat without speaking, and when he turned again toward Mornway he was surprised to find the latter watching him with a smile.

"It's good to see you, Hadley," the Governor said.

"I waited to be sent for; I knew you'd let me know when you wanted me," Shackwell replied.

"I didn't send for you on purpose. If I had, I might have asked your advice, and I didn't want to ask anybody's advice but my own." The Governor spoke steadily, but in a voice a trifle too well disciplined to be natural. "I've had a three days' conference with myself," he continued, "and now that everything is settled I want you to do me a favor."

"Yes?" Shackwell assented. The private issues of the affair were still wrapped in mystery to him, but he had never had a moment's doubt as to its public solution, and he had no difficulty in conjecturing the nature of the service he was to render. His heart ached for Mornway, but he was glad the inevitable step was to be taken without further delay.

"Everything is settled," the Governor repeated, "and I want you to notify the press that I have decided to reappoint Fleetwood."

Shackwell bounded from his seat. "Good heavens!" he ejaculated.

"To reappoint Fleetwood," the Governor repeated, "because at the present juncture of affairs he is the only man for the place. The work we began together is not finished, and I can't finish it without him. Remember the vistas opened by the Lead Trust investigation—he knows where they lead and no one else does. We must put that inquiry through, no matter what it costs us, and that is why I have sent for you to take this letter to the 'Spy.'"

Shackwell's hand drew back from the proffered envelope.

"You say you don't want my advice, but you can't expect me to go on such an errand with my eyes shut. What on earth are you driving at? Of course Fleetwood will persist in refusing."

Mornway smiled. "He did persist—for three hours. But when he left here just now he had given me his word to accept."

Shackwell groaned. "Then I am dealing with two madmen instead of one."

The Governor laughed. "My poor Hadley, you're worse than I expected. I thought you would understand me."

"Understand you? How can I, in heaven's name, when I don't understand the situation?

"The situation—the situation?" Mornway repeated slowly. "Whose? His or mine? I don't either—I haven't had time to think of them."

"What on earth have you been thinking of then?"

The Governor rose, with a gesture toward the window, through which, below the slope of the Capitol grounds, the roofs and steeples of the city spread their smoky mass to the mild air.

"Of all that is left," he said. "Of everything except Fleetwood and myself."

"Ah—" Shackwell murmured.

Mornway turned back and sank into his seat. "Don't you see that was all I had to turn to? The State—the country—it's big enough, in all conscience, to fill a good deal of a void! My own walls had grown too cramped for me, so I just stepped outside. You have no idea how it simplified matters at once. All I had to do was to say to myself: 'Go ahead, and do the best you can for the country.' The personal issue simply didn't exist."

"Yes—and then?"

"Then I turned over for three days this question of the Attorney-Generalship. I couldn't see that it was changed—how should *my* feelings have affected it? Fleetwood hasn't betrayed the State. There isn't a scar on his public record—he is still the best man for the place. My business is to appoint the best man I can find, and I can't find any one as good as Fleetwood."

"But—but—your wife?" Shackwell stammered.

The Governor looked up with surprise. Shackwell could almost have sworn that he had indeed forgotten the private issue.

"My wife is ready to face the consequences," he said.

Shackwell returned to his former attitude of incredulity.

"But Fleetwood? Fleetwood has no right to sacrifice—"

"To sacrifice my wife to the State? Oh, let us beware of big words. Fleetwood was inclined to use them at first, but I managed to restore his sense of proportion. I showed him that our private lives are only a few feet square anyhow, and that really, to breathe freely, one must get out of them into the open." He paused and broke out with sudden violence, "My God, Hadley, didn't you see that Fleetwood had to obey me?"

"Yes—I see that," said Shackwell, with reviving obstinacy. "But if you've reached such a height and pulled him up to your side it seems to me that from that standpoint you ought to get an even clearer view of the madness of your position. You say you have decided to sacrifice your own feelings and your wife's—though I'm not so sure of your right to dispose of *her* voice in the matter; but what if you sacrifice the party and the State as well, in this transcendental attempt to distinguish between private and public honor? You'll have to answer that before you can get me to carry this letter."

The Governor did not blanch under the attack.

"I think the letter will answer you," he said calmly.

"The letter?"

"Yes. It's something more than a notification of Fleetwood's reappointment." Mornway paused and looked steadily at his friend. "You're afraid of an investigation—an impeachment? Well, the letter anticipates that."

"How, in heaven's name?"

"By a plain statement of the facts. My wife has told me that she did borrow of Fleetwood. He speculated for her and made a considerable sum, out of which she repaid his loan. The 'Spy's' accusation is true. If it can be proved that my wife induced me to appoint Fleetwood, it may be argued that she sold him the appointment. But it can't be proved, and the 'Spy' won't waste its breath in trying to, because my statement will take the sting out of its innuendoes. I propose to anticipate its attack by setting forth the facts in its columns, and asking the public to decide between us. On one side is the private fact that my wife, without my knowledge, borrowed money from Fleetwood just before I appointed him to an important post; on the other side is his public record and mine. I want people to see both sides and judge between them, not in the red glare of a newspaper denunciation, but in the plain daylight of common-sense. Charges against the private morality of a public man are usually made in such a blare of headlines and cloud of mud-throwing that the voice he lifts up in his defence can not make itself heard. In this case I want the public to hear what I have to say before the yelping begins. My letter will take the wind out of the 'Spy's' sails, and if the verdict goes against me, the case will have been decided on its own merits, and not at the dictation of the writers of scare heads. Even if I don't gain my end, it will be a good thing, for once, for the public to consider dispassionately how far a private calamity should be allowed to affect a career of public usefulness, and the next man who goes through what I am undergoing may have cause to thank me if no one else does."

Shackwell sat silent for a moment, with the ring of the last words in his ears.

Suddenly he rose and held out his hand. "Give me the letter," he said.

The Governor caught him up with a kindling eye. "It's all right, then? You see, and you'll take it?"

Shackwell met his glance with one of melancholy interrogation. "I think I see a magnificent suicide, but it's the kind of way I shouldn't mind dying myself."

He pulled himself silently into his coat and put the letter into one of its pockets, but as he was turning to the door the Governor called after him cheerfully: "By the way, Hadley, aren't you and Mrs. Shackwell giving a big dinner to-morrow?"

Shackwell paused with a start. "I believe we are—why?"

"Because, if there is room for two more, my wife and I would like to be invited."

Shackwell nodded his assent and turned away without answering. As he came out of the lobby into the clear sunset radiance he saw a victoria drive up the long sweep to the Capitol and pause before the central portion. He descended the steps, and Mrs. Mornway leaned from her furs to greet him.

"I have called for my husband," she said, smiling. "He promised to get away in time for a little turn in the Park before dinner."

Printed in the United Kingdom
by Lightning Source UK Ltd.
135382UK00001B/344/P